A Time to Be Born

To every thing there is a season,
and a time to every purpose under the heaven:

A time to be born, and a time to die;
a time to plant, and a time to pluck up that which is planted;

A time to kill, and a time to heal;
a time to break down, and a time to build up;

A time to weep, and a time to laugh;
a time to mourn, and a time to dance; . . .

Ecclesiastes 3
King James Version

A Time to Be Born

by David Bell, M.D.

WILLIAM MORROW & COMPANY, INC.
NEW YORK, 1975

Printed in the United States of America.

1 2 3 4 5   79 78 77 76 75

Library of Congress Cataloging in Publication Data

Bell, David (date)
  A time to be born.

  I. Title.
PZ4.B4336Ti   [PS3552.E49]   813'.5'4   74-14648
ISBN 0-688-00332-X

Book Design by Helen Roberts

This book is dedicated to all newborn infants, for before them lie the indescribable experiences of life.

Foreword

There are so many paradoxes in medicine. Perhaps it is best to ignore the conflicting issues and emotions that may be impossible to resolve. Yet they cannot be avoided and are met daily on some level during medical practice. I wanted to write this book to explain some of these conflicts to myself. Now that the book is completed, I see I have no answers. But at least I have defined for myself some of the questions.

I am a pediatrician, having gone through the usual channels—college and four years of medical school. When I graduated with the M.D. degree, immediately I began to specialize in pediatrics, with an internship and residency devoted entirely to children's medical problems. It was in these years of training that I first assumed responsibility for the health of my patients. Experienced doctors may smile at the naïveté of my thoughts, perhaps remembering their own.

A major part of my training was in the intensive care nursery, caring for critically ill newborns. Many of the issues and conflicts in medicine are apparent when a child begins life, and the four children described in this book are infants. The case histories, and almost every event, I have seen happen at one time or another. However, for the privacy of my patients and their families, the names and stories have been changed to make individual recognition impossible. I have left out the myriad technical details involved in intensive care so the more basic issues might remain in focus. These four children represent for me the problems posed by hundreds of children, each of whom has raised doubts as to what I was doing and why.

During my work in the nursery I saw infants die. I saw many more live. I witnessed the joys and griefs and experienced them along with the parents. Yet, at the time, I could never explain fully what had happened, either to myself or to the parents. Much of what is said in this book I wish I could have shared with the parents of my patients.

Contents

part i
   Jeremy Cooper   11
part ii
   Susan Jenkins   73
part iii
   Phreddie Martin   109
part iv
   Stephen Benson   155

Glossary of Medical Terms   189

part i
Jeremy Cooper

(1)

Jeremy Cooper was born late at night. The pregnancy had been long, filled with uncounted experiences and feelings, the passing of the months marked by the movement of the child inside, the gain in weight, the backaches. Evidently, Jeremy's mother had not thought very much about the labor, and she was surprised by the intensity of the pain once it began. She and her husband came to the emergency floor, where she was examined and admitted directly to the labor room. Mr. Cooper waited in the maternity lobby, not knowing if the screams he heard were those of his wife or one of the other women in labor.

Because of the unbearable pain, Mrs. Cooper was given a narcotic, Demerol, in a dose that lessened the pain only slightly during contractions, but made her comfortable and relaxed in the intervals between them. Narcotics, like all drugs given to a pregnant woman, have an effect upon the unborn child. Because one of the side effects of a narcotic is to slow breathing, the dose used in labor is small; otherwise the infant would not be able to breathe at birth. Between the pains she slept, but with each contraction the pain and fear returned, a fear that only a woman in labor can understand.

Her blood pressure was normal, and every fifteen minutes a nurse would listen through Mrs. Cooper's abdomen to the infant's heartbeat with a fetuscope. The unborn child's heart was strong and regular. The obstetrical resident did vaginal examinations frequently to see how the baby was descending through the pelvis. As labor progressed the baby moved down through the birth canal; the labor and delivery were going nicely.

At one in the morning, Mrs. Cooper's membranes ruptured, releasing all the amniotic fluid that had surrounded the baby for the nine months of pregnancy. Usually this fluid is clear, perhaps slightly yellow in color, but her fluid was stained a dark green because of meconium, the thick.material filling the infant's digestive tract. For this reason the pediatricians were notified, and Pam and I came up to meet Mrs. Cooper. Pam was the pediatric intern and I was the pediatric resident in charge of the nursery.

Most babies pass meconium from their bowels in the first day after birth, but about 20 percent will pass meconium while still inside the womb, and this stains the amnotic fluid a black-green. We were called for two reasons. Occasionally this is a sign that the baby is in trouble, or is "distressed." If the baby's blood supply were to be cut off, for example, by the umbilical cord being compressed against the bones of the pelvis, the baby might respond by passing meconium. Secondly, if the baby were to take a breath or two before being born, this meconium would then go into the child's lungs, making it difficult to breathe at the time of birth. It is a sign in medicine that alerts us to possible difficulties and to be prepared for an emergency; but most of the time there are no problems.

I read through Mrs. Cooper's chart. The pregnancy had been normal, and although she was obese, she was in good health. This was her first pregnancy. The baby was about a week overdue, and older babies are more likely to pass meconium early without problems being present. I introduced Dr. Meehan and myself to Mrs. Cooper and, between contractions, explained to her why we had been called. Her blood pressure and temperature were normal, and the baby's heart rate was 140—normal. There were no other signs of distress, and I advised her that I did not think there would be any problems with the birth.

"Are you sure?" she asked, the fear returning as she began a contraction.

"I am fairly sure," I said.

"Dear Jesus, please make everything all right . . ." And she closed her eyes as if praying.

After the contraction passed, I explained that Pam and I would be present at the delivery just in case there were any problems. She looked somewhat relieved, but a seed of doubt had been placed in her mind, a seed which I could not, in honesty, completely remove. The nurses would call us just before the delivery, and Pam and I walked back to the nursery. It had been a fairly quiet night, but there were many things to do.

At 3 A.M. Mrs. Cooper's baby was born. A few minutes earlier she had begun to push the baby out, but there was no one around to take her to the delivery room. Another birth was going on at the time, and the obstetrical resident and the two nurses were in the delivery room with the other mother, unaware that Mrs. Cooper was pushing. The aide who was watching the other women in the labor room had gone to the supply room to get a bottle of saline. Mrs. Cooper's screams were intense but unheard. Then, with a strong push, the baby was born. As the baby was being pushed out, the umbilical cord, which had been wrapped twice about his neck, pulled tight, strangulating the infant.

Mrs. Cooper screamed with horror as the blue, limp infant lay motionless between her legs on the bed.

The nurses rushed in and, calling the obstetrician, tried to loosen the cord around the baby's neck. The obstetrical resident unwound the cord and cut it, then began to give the child artificial respiration and oxygen.

I was resting on a cot in the room next to the nursery when the phone rang. Alice, the night nurse, called out,

"Delivery room—stat," and Pam and I ran up the two flights without waiting to ask any questions. We ran into the delivery room, then finally to the labor room, where I saw a blue, limp baby being given artificial respiration. I told Pam to get the emergency cart with our equipment, and took over breathing the baby from the obstetrician.

"What happened?" I asked while listening to the heartbeat. It was slow, about twenty per minute, but the baby was not dead.

"Precipitous delivery, cord around the neck . . ."

"How long ago?" I squeezed the baby's chest evenly and gently, trying to press oxygen from the wall outlet into his lungs.

"About ten minutes."

It was clear that the artificial respiration was not working, for the baby remained unchanged with no outward sign of life. Pam arrived with the cart, and I told her to get a number 12 endotracheal tube, the laryngoscope, and to draw up some bicarb. Because air was not getting into the baby's lungs with this kind of artificial respiration, we would put a tube through his mouth directly into his airway so we could give oxygen to his lungs. Pam listened to the heartbeat, tapping it out with her finger so I could see, and I pulled the infant's head back and passed the tube down and into his trachea. I gave three or four short puffs on the tube to expand his chest, suctioned out the amniotic fluid and meconium, and attached the ambu bag to the end of the tube. As the bag was pressed, oxygen entered the baby's lungs. The blue color quickly disappeared, but the baby remained limp and was getting cold.

"Give ten ccs. of bicarb." Pam, syringe ready, injected the bicarbonate into the vein on the umbilical cord. The warmer table had been brought over, and, still squeezing the oxygen into his lungs, we lifted him onto it. Minutes passed, and although his color and heart rate had improved with the oxygen, he had not responded by struggling and beginning to breathe for himself as I had hoped he would.

He lay still on the table, the only motion that of his chest as I pushed oxygen into his lungs.

Mrs. Cooper saw a "dead" infant on the warmer table next to her bed, and she cried as we worked to save her baby's life. The resuscitation had been without many words, our actions practiced, our attention devoted only to the baby. The obstetrical resident sat with Mrs. Cooper, explaining that the baby was not dead, that his heart was still beating strongly, that he had a chance. But she stared terrified at the dead child, her firstborn.

"Call the nursery," I said as we began wheeling the warmer table out of the labor room. The oxygen was now attached to a portable tank, and as I breathed for the baby by pressing on the ambu bag, one hand holding the tube in place in his mouth, we moved down the hallway, slowly, toward the waiting elevator. Mrs. Cooper saw us disappear with her dead child as the doors closed behind us.

But the baby was not dead. He had not come back to life the way I was hoping he would, but he was not dead. I saw that he had been without oxygen for a long time, and if he recovered, he would recover slowly. I did not think about the freak tragedy that had occurred; it was not important now. All that mattered was that the baby's life be saved, that he recover quickly, begin breathing, and grow up to be a normal person. But in the elevator, for the first time I thought that he had been dead a long time, and that if he did recover, he might not be a normal person. I quickly forced the thought out of my mind, paying close attention to Baby Boy Cooper's heart rate as the elevator moved slowly down.

The elevator operator watched silently, wishing his elevator would move faster.

(2)

The nursery had been called by the delivery floor and told to expect a bad baby. No more needed to be said; the routine was enacted and preparations were hastily but methodically made. We had often joked that someday the call would be for two simultaneous sets of sick triplets, but nobody ever laughed at that—somehow it just needed to be said. One sick baby means hours and hours of frantic, desperate work, and six would be completely impossible.

Perhaps at this point it would be in order to explain something about sick infants. It has been said that the first few moments of a person's life are the most dangerous. In pediatrics there is a subspecialty called neonatology, which devotes itself entirely to the care of infants during pregnancy and around the time of birth. There is so much to know in this subspecialty area that it becomes difficult for the practicing pediatrician to keep up with the new information and impossible to have the equipment that this care demands, so special neonatal intensive care units are set up, and sick infants born at small community hospitals are transferred to the major centers. At these larger hospitals the babies are taken care of by the house officers, the pediatric interns and residents, under the watchful eyes of the chief neonatologist and his "fellow," a pediatrician training to be a chief neonatologist.

When the nursery receives a call that a sick baby is on

the way, a set disaster plan is employed. There is a special table incubator, with heating lamps suspended from the ceiling that keep the baby warm while allowing room around the table to work. It is like an operating table, always kept warm and ready, and after the call a sterile towel is placed on top of the table. The oxygen is turned on, and all nonessential items are removed from the room. The nurses then open sterile surgical sets, draw up medications in labeled syringes, and put tables in their proper places.

The trip in the elevator with Baby Boy Cooper seemed interminably long. No words were spoken. By the time we arrived in the nursery he looked a little better, his color now pink, but he was still not moving or making any attempt to breathe on his own. Because the endotracheal tube was down between his vocal cords, the baby would not have been able to cry even if he had had the strength. The door was flung open and we were inside the nursery.

The infant, flaccid and unresponsive, was carefully lifted by Pam while I huddled at his head, one hand squeezing the ambu bag, the other holding the tube in place. The transporter was taken away and he was placed on the heated table. Alice taped a wire to his skin to measure his temperature, then took over the ambu bag, not missing a single beat. With another piece of tape, I attached the tube firmly to his lips, and Pam checked to see if the tube was still in its proper place by listening to each side of the baby's chest. If the tube had been in too far, it would have gone into the right lung, and no sounds would be heard when listening to the left side of the chest. Should this happen, we would pull back slightly on the tube until air was heard well on both sides. The electrocardiogram and blood pressure machines were hooked up, and, by looking at the wall behind the baby, we could tell at a glance the heart rate, blood pressure, temperature, and other important measurements. The heart rate was low at about eighty per minute, but this was an improvement over what it had been just a few minutes earlier.

In a sense I had first met Baby Boy Cooper earlier in the evening, before he was even born, when I had talked with Mrs. Cooper. The infant was a part of her, he had a personality, and by talking to his mother, I felt I knew a little about the child. I did not then know the sex or the health or anything else about the infant, but I had a feeling about him. He was not another nameless seven-pounder but was Mrs. Cooper's baby. In that very brief meeting I'd had with her, I liked her, saddened a little that I had to make her worry, but I anticipated recognizing the child and liking him.

But I did not know the baby now. In situations like this, the infant ceases to be a person to me, and my face would not show the difference if I had been working with a struggling newborn or a bag of sand. Actually, it probably looked as if I were manipulating some clay object, making sure the wires were hooked up, the machines working well. I was an artist, my knowledge was my art, and I was doing what I had practiced. I was not thinking about the child, but instead was concentrating on the cardiac output, the blood pressure, the air exchange in the lungs. I was like a car mechanic, doing an emergency valve job on an engine. Baby Boy Cooper was just that: a baby boy, nameless, formless, almost lifeless, and I was creating as much emotional distance from the child as I could. Inside me, I guess I felt that if he died, I would rather not know him.

Once, when I was in medical school, a resident warned me, saying, "Don't get emotionally involved," about a patient I had worked with. I had talked with this patient a lot and had become quite close. When he died, I was distraught and considered giving up medicine as a career; I then understood why the resident had warned me. He had said that, to prevent future sadness, you should not become too involved with your patients. "Don't get involved" are words that stand out most in my medical training because they are just the opposite from the reasons why I wanted to go into medicine. But in some ways they are a necessity.

I am confused by this, as I cannot allow myself to forsake present emotional involvement because of some possible future grief, but on an unconscious level I do, and that is why I saw the clay in front of me, why I was busy checking the sand's blood pressure. We may just need a whole new engine if this one doesn't come around.

Perhaps this distance is a normal defense mechanism, and even healthy for both me and my patient, for it would have been impossible for me to deal with the emotionality of the situation and maintain proper medical judgment at the same time. Yet it is difficult to justify this cold, emotionless attitude by saying that it is just a normal defense.

When the child came into the nursery, a nurse automatically wrapped one of his feet in a hot towel to prepare for a blood gas measurement. By heating up the foot for ten minutes, the blood becomes mostly arterial (blood with a high amount of oxygen) rather than venous (blood returning to the heart after having used up its oxygen). After making a small cut on the side of the warmed foot, the arterial blood is collected in special small tubes that prevent blood from clotting and then taken to the blood gas machine for various measurements. These measurements are necessary for "enlightened" management of the critically ill infant. First, it is important to know how much oxygen is in the blood. Infants with lung or heart disease will have a low blood oxygen and will need oxygen to correct the problem temporarily. But if the oxygen in the blood is too high, then this also can be dangerous, as it, like any drug, can have side effects. If the infant is breathing pure oxygen and has no lung disease, then the amount in the blood will be very high and, if continued for a period of time, can cause its own set of problems, blindness being one example.

Secondly, it is important to measure the carbon dioxide in the blood to see if the patient is being ventilated properly. Baby Boy Cooper was not breathing by himself. We were breathing for him with a tube and an ambu bag, and we had to be sure we were doing it in a similar manner as he would, were he able to. The human body does such complicated things automatically that it is hard to realize just how difficult these things are until you try to imitate them. Human physiology is a balance, and when something is not working properly, then many other bodily systems can be affected.

Thirdly, the machine measures the amount of acid in the blood. Normally, the pH (amount of acid) is about 7.40, but if circulation is poor, more acid accumulates. Sodium bicarbonate is given in this circumstance because it neutralizes the acid. We gave Baby Boy Cooper a dose of bicarbonate on the delivery floor because almost all babies in this sort of trouble are "acidotic." But if you give too much, or if the infant does not need the bicarbonate, this can be dangerous. The dose we gave on the delivery floor was a guess, as we had no measurements to go by, and, hopefully, with experience the guess is usually correct. By measuring the blood pH on the blood gas machine, you get a certain number, say 6.95 if things are bad, and with this figure you can calculate how much bicarbonate to give. In modern medicine the art of guessing is frowned upon, and the image of the general practitioner who stands by the bedside and guesses a certain dose is not held in esteem. But then again, the general practitioner does not have Terrible Tillie.

Tillie is the blood gas machine. She is the most beautiful, fragile, and dangerous machine I ever hope to meet. The sign of status in nurseries today is the blood gas machine. If you don't have one in your nursery, it can't be an intensive care nursery, it can't be big-time. These machines are very expensive—I have no idea how much they cost—and they are unbelievably complicated to work, at least to me. During the day there is a technician who runs the machine, but not at night. All the residents know how to run Tillie, and everyone is terrified of her. She is the adopted child of our neonatology fellow, John, and he spends much of his time cleaning out her tubes, replacing her chemicals, and threatening us should we break her.

And she is very easy to break. I am afraid of Tillie because if I should break her, as I have often done, I will cost the hospital untold sums of money, ruin the nursery's prestige, and, worst of all, incur the wrath of John. Sometimes, late at night, I want to accuse John of caring more for his machine than for my patient.

It took about ten minutes to get everything organized and Baby Boy Cooper stable. His color was pink, and it looked as if he was going to live, although he was not yet breathing for himself. I told Pam to drop in a venous tube and take over while I did a blood gas. "Dropping a tube" means to place a small plastic catheter into the vein of the umbilical cord, through which intravenous fluids and medications are given. This needed to be done by the time I had finished with the blood gas measurements, as we would probably have to give more bicarbonate. I made a cut on the warmed heel and carried off several small tubes of blood to Tillie.

Tillie worked nicely, and five minutes later I ran back into the nursery with the results. Pam had finished putting in the line, and the IV (intravenous fluids) was running well. We gave a small dose of bicarbonate and lowered the amount of oxygen the baby was taking in almost to room air. Alice's arm was nearly paralyzed by now, and Pam took over breathing for the baby, squeezing the ambu bag at regular intervals. I went to the telephone: Baby Boy Cooper was now stable enough for me to call John.

The blood gas measurements unfortunately confirmed what I had suspected and feared. Because the amount of oxygen in the baby's blood was almost normal, there could be no lung disease preventing the oxygen from getting into the blood. But the child was unable to breathe for himself, and in the absence of lung disease, this meant there had to be brain damage to those areas of the brain which regulate breathing. Moreover, the baby's limp posture suggested brain damage, and the nature of the tragedy around the baby's birth made this diagnosis hard to dispute. But my mind ran over the question, "Could only ten or fifteen minutes of anoxia [oxygen deprivation] cause this severe a problem?"

John hates to be awakened at three-thirty in the morning. There was no reason why sick babies couldn't be born at eight o'clock instead. I called him, expecting his angry voice and hearing it after half of the first ring. I explained the situation briefly while he listened in silence. He said that he would be in and hung up. I felt that I had again disappointed him because the baby was sick. John is on call every day and night throughout the year and always comes in for emergencies. However, he knows more about sick babies than I do, and I was happy that he would be coming in to help. We have our differences, but John is an excellent neonatology fellow. If he should not know the answer to a problem, then he calls his boss, Dr. Williams, who is the director of the nursery, the Chief of Neonatology. But John and Dr. Williams act as advisers only: I always follow their advice, but Baby Boy Cooper was my patient.

By this time the infant was beginning to take a few gasps on his own, not vigorously, but he was starting to move a little, open his eyes, sometimes try to breathe against the tube. His color was good, but he was "floppy," meaning the tone of his muscles was not good. This was an ominous sign, but I told myself it was too early to think about the future. A hematocrit was drawn (a blood test to measure the blood volume), and blood was sent to the laboratory for routine tests, all of which turned out to be normal. The x-ray technician came over to take a chest x-ray, angry to have to come in the middle of the night. The x-ray was normal, showing the endotracheal tube to be in its proper place in the airway, clear lungs, and normal heart shape and size.

John walked into the nursery and said, "Well, how's our baby?" Mrs. Cooper, now crying in some dark recovery room, could no longer claim possession of the child. She caused us this problem by getting pregnant, and we had done all this work in the hope of saving the baby's life.

She had seen the child for only a moment, and we had been with the infant for almost two hours, and she would not be able to see her child until we allowed her to. Pam and I proudly announce the birth of a son, Baby Boy Cooper, a child who has become our responsibility through a completely preventable freak accident. Now grandfather John is adopting the baby. But because we are such selfless doctors, we will give the baby back if we can fix him.

We had repeated the blood gas measurements and had the results of the blood tests and the x-rays. Despite the baby's not being able to breathe, everything else looked in reasonably good condition, considering. Pam continued to push the oxygen-air mixture into his lungs while he tried to take an occasional breath. John surveyed the blood pressure and EKG machines, asked about Tillie, looked at the blood results, complained about the mess the room was in (there were papers, dried blood, used syringes lying about), but was generally pleased that we had kept the baby alive. Baby Boy Cooper, the endotracheal tube coming from his mouth, seemed to gaze over toward John silently.

John was fully awake now, bustling with energy and ready for the challenge. Pam and I were tired, our minds slowed with physical fatigue and lack of sleep. The knowledge that there would be twelve more hours of intensive work weighed on our minds, making us feel guilty about our selfishness. The immediate emergency was over, the baby now two hours old, but the real work was just beginning. Just a cup of coffee, a cigarette, please, my mind cried out, but the baby was waiting, so we readied the respirator.

(3)

Baby Boy Cooper had begun to breathe on his own, but the breaths were not very deep, and there were long periods in between. We tried to see how well he could do by disconnecting the ambu bag and allowing him to breathe through the tube. We placed a plastic hood filled with oxygen around his head and watched him carefully for ten minutes. His breathing was irregular and shallow, and at one point he did not take a breath for about thirty seconds, this being called "apnea." We helped him start breathing again by slapping the soles of his feet, which startled him into taking another breath. At the end of the ten minutes we warmed his heel with a hot towel and again measured the blood gases. It was clear, however, that he could not yet live on his own, that he needed assistance with breathing.

During the time that Baby Boy Cooper was on his own, Pam and I had a chance to do a careful examination. We felt for his fontanelles, measured his head circumference, felt for his liver and kidneys, and tested his reflexes. The neurological examination, which tests brain and nerve functions, was very abnormal, and silently, as Pam and I felt the baby, we both realized the extraordinary amount of brain damage present. This we had really known all along but had not wanted to admit to ourselves. The infant, if he lived, could have very severe brain damage.

When I first arrive at an emergency, one unspoken question enters my mind: "What will be the consequences if I should be successful in bringing this child back to life?" I had asked myself this question with Baby Boy Cooper, and now I was beginning to see what these consequences would be. I do not know if other doctors ask themselves this question, for it is not something we talk about very much. We seem much more concerned for the practical, mechanical aspects of how to perform a resuscitation rather than the illusive, intangible morality of whether a resuscitation should be done. I believe everyone has his or her own set of ethics about this question, but I regret not knowing if my own standards would be considered ethical by other people.

But the ethical and moral problems are enormous. If you are present when a presumably healthy baby stops breathing, and with an efficient, rapid resuscitation the child is revived and goes on to be subsequently well, there is no moral dilemma. There is no question that the resuscitation was correct, and, indeed, it would have been criminal not to do it. In that situation the doctor has saved the child and allowed fifty, seventy, ninety years of life. The doctor helped God out a little in His indecision.

Suppose, however, that the infant had been "dead" for three-quarters of an hour before you arrive, and after a successful resuscitation, although this may be unlikely, the child is brought back to life. After being dead for this long, there would be severe brain damage, and the child may then lead his or her life as a helpless cripple, never gaining the mental age of one year, causing enormous disruption of family life, perhaps being sent to the back wards of a state hospital to live out the tenuous, frail life allowed. These children develop serious medical problems: kidney disease, seizures, custodial care costing the parents untold sums of money, perhaps depriving other children in the family of the life that was hoped for them. Moreover, because the child's life was saved, the parents are unable to mourn the tragedy that has befallen the family.

Perhaps it was "God's will" that the infant die, and the doctor altered nature in such a way as to cause the family and the patient suffering. Is it morally right to alter nature in such a way?

There are, of course, infinite middle roads. Are you justified in making a decision not to resuscitate a "dead" infant, or in even asking the question? Are you able to draw a line, a time limit, and if so, where? After being "dead" for fifteen minutes, some children lead normal lives or are only mildly retarded. When a child has not breathed for half an hour, yet the heart still beats, is it morally justifiable to stand by and watch the infant die, when you, as the physician, might be able to save the physiologic life? In these situations you pretend you are God's messenger, duly authorized to make a decision, then hope you are right.

The essential question is whether life under any circumstances is preferable to death. I feel an indefinable guilt about saving a life after twenty minutes of death because I know of the consequences that usually follow such an act. I do not mean mild mental retardation, or mild cerebral palsy, but profound retardation where life as we know it does not exist. Is it better to live such a way or to have died? As a physician, I am trained to see death as a personal failure. But is life under these circumstances any less of a defeat?

I also feel guilt at the mere idea that I am weighing the life of a child against the knowledge that he will not grow up to be intelligent. Life is precious, and who am I to decide that being severely retarded is worse than not living at all?

There is no single answer to these questions. The decision to resuscitate a dead child ultimately rests with the beliefs of the physician who arrives at the emergency. The unanswered question is what does the patient want? How do you ask a newborn whether he or she wants to come back to life in spite of the possible consequences? How do you ask a ten-year-old retarded child, who cannot see or hear or think, whether he was glad he was resuscitated as an infant?

My personal belief is that I am unable to stand by while a child dies if there is a chance that the infant might be normal if resuscitated. In the moment of decision I quickly look for the cause of the emergency, and underlying illnesses, and the chances for recovery. But there are so many variables, and most of the time it is impossible to guess at the outcome. I would tend to err on the side of life, recognizing that I was "responsible" for saving hopelessly retarded children, rather than wonder if I had let a child die—a child who could have been normal.

I believe in the integrity of nature, yet science is an addition to nature and has become part of it. I have seen life as a healthy person, but perhaps a severely retarded child is happier with life than I. I do not know. But a decision has to be made, and although I don't want to make it, I have to, one way or another. To walk away is to make a decision. The decision I have made is that if I do not know the results of a given situation, I hope for the best and do all I can. Being young and inexperienced, I do not know that this is right. Whatever the decision, I feel guilty and have to fight ambivalence.

The decision was made with Baby Boy Cooper. In about two seconds I recognized the alternatives and decided to resuscitate him. I could not ask Mrs. Cooper for advice. In medicine, because we are detached, we are less able to understand the implications of our decisions for the family and the patient. But there is no time in a situation like this to allow the parents one month to come to understand the decision and make a thoughtful choice. You have five seconds, no more, and once the decision is made, you stick to it.

It seems ironic that the doctors who make the life-and-death decisions are often the least experienced. At night just the intern and resident are in the nursery, and when these situations arise, the experience and judgment of a Dr. Williams or a John are not available. It seems a little easier talking about what should have been done sitting in an armchair two days later, but at the moment a child stops breathing, the decision to resuscitate is often made by a doctor who has little experience or knowledge of the consequences.

Soon I will finish my formal training, having gained the experience and, I hope, some judgment, but then I will no longer have to make as many of these decisions, for the new interns and residents will be in the nursery. Perhaps because no one wants to assume the responsibility for the decisions, the buck is passed to the newest, least experienced doctors.

I don't want this responsibility. I don't know God, or even know if He exists, and I certainly don't want to pretend to be God. In medical school, a resident I knew carried a card around, one half saying "God," the other half saying "me." When an accident patient was resuscitated successfully, he would place a checkmark on the "me" side; if the patient died, a check under "God." I am embarrassed by this sickness in a fellow doctor, but I recognize that I might be fighting God also, and I don't know how to get out of it.

After I made the decision to resuscitate Baby Boy Cooper I did not want to recognize the obvious signs of brain damage, knowing they would bring up all those complicated, ambivalent questions. But the baby cared little about any questions that I might have and went on showing the signs. Now both Pam and I stared helplessly.

But babies are resilient, more so than older children or adults. Often what seems to be a terrible insult may not result in much permanent damage. With Baby Boy Cooper it was too early to know for sure, but the signs already present were ominous. And the longer he remained in this condition, the less hopeful we could become. The baby had been without oxygen for an unknown amount of time, probably fifteen minutes at the most. To me this did not seem enough of an insult to be causing this severe a problem. His lungs were normal, and the difficulty in breathing was because of brain injury, yet ten to fifteen minutes did not justify this much apnea. I believed there was probably something else happening.

When an infant's brain is without oxygen, an intracranial hemorrhage, or bleeding into the brain, will occasionally result, and this bleeding will, in itself, cause further destruction of brain tissue, thus adding to the initial injury. I felt that the strangulation probably caused a brain hemorrhage, and the combination of the two resulted in the flaccid, apneic baby we now saw. Unfortunately, there is little treatment for an intracranial hemorrhage at this stage, and it was more appropriate to ignore it and get on to more pressing work. We would find out if there had been any bleeding in due time.

After those ten minutes of rather unsuccessful breathing on the baby's own, I carried the arterial blood to Tillie. I fitted all the little tubes correctly, turned the right knobs, but Tillie broke. She always seemed to break whenever John came in. It looked as if some of the blood had clotted inside the machine, and with great fear I walked back to tell John. I wanted one last cigarette before I got fired, but there was no time. John accepted the news exactly as I had suspected he would: I had done something wrong, I was an idiot. He went in to try to console Tillie, and I went to get the respirator. Pam smiled as she continued to breathe Baby Boy Cooper by hand. She had never really liked Tillie either.

The respirator is another huge complicated machine, this one designed to breathe for a baby. The same tube that was in the infant's lungs would now be connected to plastic hosing that disappeared inside the machine. The machine would then mix the correct amount of oxygen and air and deliver the proper volume at the proper pressure at the proper time intervals. There were formulas and dials on the machine for each of these measurements. I put on the sterile hosing, put water in the jars, plugged the respirator in, and waited for John. The machine had two options: it could breathe for the patient automatically, or merely assist with the breathing. I put the machine to "automatic," as Baby Boy Cooper was not strong enough for assist. With a piece of adhesive tape I wrapped the tube firmly and attached it to the baby's upper lip. Then I listened carefully to his chest to be sure the tube had not moved.

John returned, having repaired Tillie, and we connected the respirator to the tube in the baby's mouth. As Pam rested her aching arm, I was sympathetic, remembering when I had been an intern. In two years Pam would get the thinking jobs, and her intern would do the manual labor. The machine began its steady monotone hum, broken every two seconds by the sound of air being pushed into Baby Boy Cooper's chest.

When a baby is "on the respirator," it is important to measure the blood gases frequently. Because his heel was becoming a little macerated from the cuts we were making, we decided to put a catheter into his umbilical artery. Arterial blood may be drawn for the tests from this catheter, and when it is not being used for that purpose, it can deliver intravenous fluids—glucose and water. To put a catheter into the umbilical artery is tricky: it is like a surgical operation, and everything must be kept sterile to prevent infection. Pam and I put on sterile gowns, hats, and masks, changing gloves after cleaning off the umbilical cord with iodine. There are two small arteries and one vein in the umbilical cord. The catheter was easy to put into the large vein, but the artery was another story.

With a scalpel we cut through the jelly-like cord, exposing the two small arteries. Pam had never done this before, so I explained it step by step while she threaded the tiny catheter into the artery. Nature has provided for the inexperience of interns by having two arteries in the cord, so if she were unable to accomplish the task on her artery, there would be an unused one for me to try. Interns learn in medicine by doing these procedures; there is no other way. She worked slowly and methodically, gently sliding the catheter in until it came to the aorta, the major artery of the body, and through this until it was almost to the heart. At one point the catheter became stuck in one of the smaller branches of the umbilical artery, so we turned the tubing in such a way as to free it. By measuring the catheter beforehand, we knew how far to insert it.

During this procedure, the baby had been on the warmer table, heated from the ceiling to 98.8°. This meant the air around the table was also at 98.8°. We were dressed in our nursery clothes and the heavy gowns, hats, and masks. Sweat poured from every part of us, and because we wore sterile gloves, we couldn't touch anything. The salt burned our eyes; the heat was suffocating. Our clothes were drenched and our backs ached, but none of this was mentioned because of the seriousness of the situation. The baby was still close to death—it was hardly a time to talk about personal inconveniences. If one small drop of sweat were to fall onto the catheter, disaster could result. But I could not stop myself from sweating. I tried to predict when a drop of sweat was about to fall, and at the proper moment I would lean away from the table and let it fall onto the floor. Occasionally Alice would wipe my forehead, asking me politely to stop sweating.

It took about twenty minutes to place the catheter and hook it up to the IV solution. The plastic tubing was sewn into the umbilical cord so it could not be pulled out accidentally. The tube that had been placed in the vein earlier was then removed, as there was no need for two tubes, and a bandage was placed over the stump. Another x-ray showed that the catheter was in its proper place just below the heart. We moved away from the warmer table, dropped off our soaked gowns, and breathed some of the cool room air.

Baby Boy Cooper was alive and, for the moment, stable. He had made some progress in that he would now try to take an occasional breath, but not the sort of progress we were pleased with. The respirator breathed for him, and intravenous fluids ran into his umbilical artery. He was now about four hours old, yet somehow seemed much older. As I looked at him, I realized that I had become part of his life, and he, mine. I was too tired to imagine what our relationship would be like over the coming hours, days, or years.

It was dawn, and John was talking about one of the other babies in the nursery. But I could not listen—I wondered if Baby Boy Cooper could possibly recover. Pam stayed with the baby, and I walked upstairs to talk with his mother.

(4)

When I arrived at the delivery floor, I saw Frank, the obstetrical resident on duty, sitting at the desk. I knew Frank pretty well, so we wasted no time starting to talk—we were both tired. How could I tell him that he shouldn't have let the baby strangle? He was a good doctor, and at the time he had been delivering another baby; he was, in one sense, not at fault. The two nurses had been busy assisting with the delivery, working hard—it was not their fault. The aide had been getting the bottle of saline, and Mrs. Cooper was frightened and drugged. The hospital had been trying to hire more nurses, but nobody wanted the night shift. It was not the hospital's fault. It was nobody's fault, yet it was an unbelievable, inexcusable tragedy. Baby Boy Cooper should now have been a healthy, sleeping newborn. There was little I could say, but as I told him how the baby was doing, I saw that he had assumed responsibility for the accident. He showed me into Mrs. Cooper's room.

She had been given a sedative but was not asleep. She recognized me at once, and propped herself up on the pillows with apprehension. "Is he all right?" she asked.

"He is alive," I answered, sitting beside her, "but he is in very critical condition."

"Oh, thank God he's alive. Thank Jesus . . . just as long as he's alive." There were a few moments of silence, and she lay back on the pillows.

"He is not able to breathe for himself," I began slowly, "and I do not yet know if he will live. He is unable to breathe for himself because of damage to his brain. Right now I can only hope he will recover; it is too early to tell."

Mrs. Cooper lay with her eyes closed, crying softly. She seemed not to be listening as I explained about his condition and the respirator. Then she interrupted and, looking toward me, said, "Please, Doctor, do everything you can . . . he will be all right, I know it."

"I will do what I can," I answered, and as our eyes met, I felt that she had asked for and I had given a promise. I wanted to say that he would be well, but I couldn't. I wanted to explain what brain damage meant, but I couldn't. "I'm sorry this had to happen," I said finally.

The curtain was drawn, separating Mrs. Cooper from the four other sleeping mothers. She cried softly, and as I stood up to leave she said, "His name is Jeremy."

"I will tell your husband about Jeremy." The child was no longer an anonymous male child; he was Jeremy Cooper.

I thought that Mrs. Cooper had been unable to accept the reality of what I had told her, perhaps because of my own inability to accept it. But her denial was also different. It was more than a desperate attempt to avoid the bad news; it was an expression of courage and faith. I had said what had to be said. It was now time for the words to settle. She would slowly, perhaps over a period of years, recognize the reality much more clearly than I possibly could.

Mr. Cooper was waiting in the lobby. Frank had told him what had happened, but I did not know specifically what had been said. I knew that I would be completely honest with him, making no excuses—it was the very least I could do. I described in detail what had happened and told him about Jeremy's condition in a similar way as I had told his wife. They shared their grief separately, each afraid to cry in front of the other. When he became strong again, he went into his wife's room.

It was impossible for me to know the grief they felt. I felt hollow and cold, not knowing what to say to make them feel better, knowing they had to grieve and that I shouldn't say anything at all. I was like Tillie, tired and fragile, giving out cold, despairing information, then going silent. I wanted to be black like the Coopers, to have something in common with them, but I was a rich white doctor, and they were poor ghetto patients. I wanted to say that I understood, but I had never known grief like this. However, in a way I cannot describe, I did feel close to them. As I walked back downstairs, I wished this empathy could make the child recover.

By the time I arrived in the nursery, Pam had finished writing the note in Jeremy's chart and had done some of the other routine things that were waiting. John talked about the physiology of anoxia, but Pam wasn't listening. John was unable to tell when people were listening to him. I checked the dials on the respirator, the EKG, the blood pressure, and was setting up to take bacteriologic cultures when Alice called me over to the table. Jeremy's left leg was shaking in a rhythmic manner; he was having a convulsion. John came over and we watched silently. This was evidence of brain damage that was hard to deny.

When the seizure stopped, we took samples of blood and urine for culture. A spinal tap was done for two reasons: first, to see if there could possibly be a bacterial infection causing the seizure, and secondly, to see if there had been bleeding into the brain. We disconnected the respirator, turned Jeremy on his side, breathing for him with the ambu bag again, and Pam inserted the needle into his spine. The spinal fluid was bright red, and we instantly knew there had been massive bleeding into his brain. The chances of his living were only fair, and the chances of his growing up to be a normal child were just about zero. John began talking about intracranial hemorrhages in a distracted voice.

Now we knew, and we were helpless to do anything about it. The only treatment was time; either the bleeding stopped and the baby lived, or the bleeding continued and he died. I listened to Jeremy's heart and lungs, but I wanted to cry. If the bleeding stopped and the tissues started to heal, then perhaps he would live, but he might be living without the thinking parts of his brain. There was nothing to do except wait, making sure the machines were working correctly. I walked slowly into the next room and lit a cigarette, the first in many hours, my exhausted mind wondering if I had done the right thing in bringing this infant back to life.

John came in and sat on the cot beside me. "What's the matter?" he asked.

"I am just tired . . . that's all," I answered, astounded that he did not know. When he started talking about one of the other babies in the nursery I realized that he knew what the matter was—that was why he had come in to talk with me. He just couldn't find the words.

"I'm sad because of that baby," I interrupted.

"I know how you feel," he answered, "but you get used to that sort of thing."

To get used to that sort of thing is to be really dead inside, but I was too tired to explain.

At seven o'clock, Emily, the other resident, and Steve, the other intern, came into the nursery, and the nurses changed shifts. It was Emily's turn to bring in the coffee and doughnuts, a ritual that was never violated. I had been looking forward to the coffee for six hours, and if she had forgotten, I would have gone berserk. But she didn't forget—she had often been in the same place I was in now.

"How was your night?" Emily asked cheerfully as she walked into the nurses' station. But she saw and heard the respirator and instantly knew the answer to her question. She turned back and, without waiting for the answer, began to talk about what she had done with her night off, trying to free our minds of the nursery and remind us that there was another world outside that we would get to see for ourselves that night. This was also part of the routine; the refreshed intern and resident do psychotherapy on the on-duty people. Also, we were friends.

But in spite of the exhaustion and unhappiness we were feeling, there was also a sense of accomplishment. If we had done the right thing in bringing Jeremy back to life, we had done it well. I told myself that there had been no other choice possible at the time, but that "if" was a nagging, unspoken question in the back of our inexperienced minds.

While we drank our coffee, we explained to Emily and Steve all the details of the night. It was the best coffee I have ever tasted, and as I became more refreshed, the events of the evening moved into memory. Now the day could begin. The presence of the other team added new energy, and although we wouldn't be leaving for another eight hours, there was an end in sight. Emily, because she was rested, would be in charge today. Pam and I were almost useless, but we could do the routine things, such as write notes in the charts, examine healthy babies, send off blood tests. In short, we would do everything that required little or no judgment. In another twenty-four hours we would be rested and Emily and Steve would do the "scut work." It was the cycle: thirty-four hours on duty, fourteen off, thirty-four on, and so on. Weekends and holidays were just regular days—nothing interrupted this schedule. We had four months of the nursery, two months at a time. A night on duty when it was quiet enough to sleep was rare. There was a legend that it had once happened three nights in a row.

I took Emily and Steve to Jeremy and explained the respirator settings and blood gas results. We went over the x-rays carefully and reviewed the results of the other blood tests. Emily took over, beginning by carefully examining Jeremy. I felt like the losing pitcher of a baseball game, but she was a good pediatrician and would take excellent care of the baby. I went downstairs to the showers.

(5)

During the morning, while I walked absently around doing little things, Jeremy stayed about the same. Emily made a few changes in the respirator settings, lowering the amount of added oxygen so the machine was delivering regular room air. Blood was drawn for calcium and magnesium levels on the remote chance that they might be causing the seizures, but they were normal. Em looked for everything treatable that she could think of, but there was nothing. We just had to wait and see if Jeremy recovered. He was tried off the respirator after work rounds, but he quickly stopped breathing and turned blue. He was not ready for life without the respirator. Occasionally he would open his eyes and gaze up at the ceiling as if to ask some imponderable question.

At eleven o'clock we had "visit rounds." By this time most of the routine nursery work had been completed, and it was time to sit with the "visit" (visiting professor) and discuss any interesting cases or problems that had come along during the past day. Our visit at the time happened to be Dr. Williams, the chief neonatologist. Pam and I were not looking forward to visit rounds because we were so tired, and because Dr. Williams always knew when you were not paying attention. Being tired was no excuse; you weren't allowed to mention it because it was only a minor personal inconvenience, having no place in Dr. Williams' nursery. He had been a resident many years ago, and he didn't remember being tired. The real problem was that we were sitting in soft, comfortable chairs, and the low tones of abstract discussion were quite conducive for sleep. For this reason I arranged to have two of my friends telephone me, so I had an excuse to leave the room and wake up.

Dr. Williams, of course, knew all about Jeremy, probably because John had told him earlier. John rarely reported to his boss in front of us because he wanted it to seem as if he were making all the decisions. But Dr. Williams also had an innate sense of what was happening in the nursery all the time, whether he was there or not.

He walked into the conference room and the usual pleasantries were exchanged. He liked to think that everyone enjoyed working in his nursery, and part of our responsibility was to look enthusiastic about the learning experience we were having. "I hear you were pretty busy last night," he said, sinking into his usual chair.

"Yes," I said. When I was tired, my answers were very short and I used the extra strength making the appropriate facial expressions.

"Well, why don't you tell us about it?"

I then described in detail what had happened the previous night. I spoke as if I were talking into a tape recorder, trying to make every word exact, because otherwise I would be asked about it. This exact language is an art perfected by tired interns and residents because it does not permit questions. When you are this tired, you aim to have as few questions asked as possible. Steve and Emily knew what to do: they posed intriguing questions to John and Dr. Williams; they picked up the conversation, allowing Pam and me to rest. Tomorrow we would help them out on visit rounds.

Pam and I felt we had done a good job with the mechanical aspects of the resuscitation. When you have made mistakes, even small ones, visit rounds are painful but educational experiences, as these mistakes are discussed in front of everybody. Medicine, like other jobs, works partly because of fear—you do things right not just because of your patient, but because of what might be said to you on visit rounds. The education process seems to be based on the principle that if your patient dies it is your fault and could have been prevented.

Death is rarely viewed in our nursery as a natural process. If a baby dies, there is a reason for it: usually someone has done something wrong. If a five-month-old preemie is born and dies, it was someone's fault because the baby shouldn't have been born that early. If Jeremy had died last night, Pam and I would have been responsible along with the obstetrician. Occasionally interns and residents fall apart and cry during visit rounds because of guilt, and this is considered poor taste. The mechanism of survival is to create an intellectual distance between yourself and the patient. "Ah, yes, the death was caused by too much bicarbonate . . . I will have to remember that in the future." Otherwise you go completely crazy, a very embarrassing weakness.

But the guilt is real. If, for example, a doctor makes a mistake and kills a baby by giving too much of a drug, the responsibility for this becomes verbally apparent during visit rounds. The doctor must learn from the mistake and not repeat it, and for this reason the rounds are good. Yet that error will always be on that doctor's conscience—someone smarter could have saved the patient.

Dr. Williams was very good with words, for he had been a professor for many years, spending much of his time writing articles for medical journals and giving lectures. Because of this ability with words, you find yourself agreeing with things you really disagree with. Also, because it takes so much energy to disagree, you think, "What's the use," and this gives Dr. Williams the comfortable feeling that everyone agrees with him.

The rounds proceeded rather smoothly, and we were given a rare compliment, that we had done the resuscitation quickly and efficiently. During the rounds, the question of whether we were correct to resuscitate the baby was not brought up. We went into the nursery and over to the heating table, where Dr. Williams examined Jeremy. He pointed out the signs of brain damage, quizzed us about the respirator settings, and asked the question, "Suppose this baby does not come off the respirator?"

By this, he was asking if we would stop the machine if the child did not learn how to breathe for himself. There are not enough respirators for everyone to go through life with one, and even if there were, Jeremy had so much brain damage that he wouldn't be "worth it." He was just a baby, a defective baby, and therefore his worth was less; it is all right to pull the plug on a baby like this. You can't save everybody. But Dr. Williams would not be the one to pull the plug, nor would he have to explain this to the parents.

No one answered the question because an answer was not really called for. He had just wanted to make sure that everyone was being realistic about the situation, and the depressed silence that followed assured him that everyone was. At that time Jeremy had another seizure, shaking his right arm and leg like an outraged lady whose purse had been stolen. Dr. Williams talked about seizures and the drugs used to control them. He had not seen an anoxic seizure like this in several weeks.

Visit rounds ended at twelve-thirty and Dr. Williams and John left the nursery. There had been no other sick children born since Jeremy, so Pam and I had a chance to rest. We went over to get some lunch while Em and Steve covered the nursery. We decided to try to get out early in the afternoon if it did not get busy.

After lunch we returned to the non-thinking jobs that waited to be done. If something turned up that required a decision, I asked Emily what to do. We were equals in education, but when I was this tired, she was a lot sharper than I. When Em is tired, I make the decisions. The really major decisions we check out with John. Over the past few years I have come to feel that the patient's greatest danger is the physician's lack of sleep. No patient would stand for a drunken doctor, but is it any better if the doctors are unable to make decisions because they haven't slept for two days?

So far Pam and I had been working for about thirty hours without sleep and there would be another four before going home. If by bad luck two sick babies were transferred in from another hospital, we could not go home, but would work until all the patients were stable. The longest I have worked is about seventy hours, with one or two short naps in the circumcision room. If I had made a mistake and been sued, I would spend my life paying off the debt without being able to remember what I had done wrong. But there are not enough doctors to provide good medical care; there would not be enough even if every doctor worked the same hours as house officers.

(6)

Jeremy improved little during the day. We knew that he had extensive brain damage because of the strangulation and intracranial bleeding, and that this brain damage was the cause of the seizures, his not being able to breathe or move like a normal newborn baby. We saw these things, not knowing what they would mean in the years to come. We wondered whether Jeremy would ever be able to walk and talk like other children, whether he would feel a lifetime of chagrin because he was retarded. Pam and I saw Jeremy not just as a newborn, but as a child ten years old, and we were sad. Why did nature and chance so recklessly choose this one infant as one of the retarded, crippled children of the world?

Our therapy was entirely supportive. There was no magic in any of our drugs or machines that could improve things; the magic was in allowing time for Jeremy to heal himself. Yet magic is such a hollow word, for the healing could not possibly be complete. Time was the only treatment, and the machines were keeping him alive so that he could have time. How severe was this injury really? Perhaps in a week Jeremy would be much like other children. Every doctor hears of one case where some insurmountable damage was healed, the patient going on to lead a near normal life. These were the fantasies of hope that lay before me, and I struggled to separate the fantasies from reality. Jeremy would improve, I knew that, and he would probably learn to breathe for himself. We were waiting for the obvious signs, hoping for them.

There was some improvement during the day, however small. There were periods of up to ten minutes when Jeremy would breathe by himself, the respirator disconnected. It was a good sign, for we knew that the longer he needed the respirator, the poorer his chance of survival. But this small advance was set back by the posture he was beginning to show. His fists were clenched tightly and his muscles were becoming stiff. His seizures were occurring very frequently, despite the high doses of phenobarbital and dilantin we were giving him. Blood gases were done, as were tests for blood sugar, jaundice, and others. Because Jeremy had an umbilical artery catheter in place, we gave him high doses of antibiotics to try to prevent an infection. He was fed through his catheter with a solution of glucose and electrolytes. We gave him several small transfusions to replace the blood being drawn out for tests. His other body systems were functioning well; none of the dreaded kidney, liver, or bleeding problems had developed. His heart was beating regularly and strongly.

The sign over his warmer table said Jeremy Cooper. . . .

At two in the afternoon Mr. and Mrs. Cooper knocked at the nursery door. I went into the hall and said hello, showing them toward the small sitting room next to the nursery.

"How are you feeling now?" I asked them.

"We are well," Mrs. Cooper replied stiffly. "How is the baby?"

We talked about Jeremy for a half hour. I told them he was still on the respirator, explaining that he had definitely had an intracranial hemorrhage and that he had developed seizures.

"We believe that he will be all right—we have faith in God." As Mrs. Cooper spoke, hope lifted her eyes, and there was a strength in her voice.

I had tried to prepare them as to what their baby would look like: wires attached to his arms and legs for the EKG machine, a temperature probe taped to his skin, a tube down his throat attached to the respirator, blood pressure cuffs, a catheter in his umbilical cord. And Jeremy, lying immobile on his back on the heating table. But there is no way to prepare, and the Coopers held their breath when they saw their firstborn on the center table. We were silent as they tried to accept the vision before them as their son. Jeremy stirred from his position slightly. Mrs. Cooper repeated that he would be well and abruptly turned and left the nursery.

I was very sad. There was no way I could have prevented all this from happening, but it should have been prevented. I could not repair Jeremy's mind; I could only keep his body alive.

Who was my patient? Jeremy, still on the danger list, was the patient to whom I gave the medicines, using the seven years of medical experience I had gained. I wrote notes in his record, asked for neurological consultations, did blood tests. But I was unable to talk with him for he was a newborn, only one day old. Yet he, like all newborns, was unique, not just because he had a certain disease process, but because the shape of his eyes was gentle, much like his mother's. I saw that I was beginning to know this infant as an individual, unable to maintain the emotionless distance I had tried hard to create.

I stood at the side of the table for a long time after Jeremy's parents left the nursery. I watched him open his eyes, occasionally struggling against the respirator that was breathing for him. He would move his arms and legs slowly, and he would have seizures involving one arm or just a couple of fingers. The nurses would walk by, saying little, involved in taking care of the other fifteen sick babies. Pam came over, and we looked at Jeremy in silence. She told me that we should go home and get some sleep, but I could not yet leave. It wasn't that busy, but the turmoil in my mind held me in the nursery. We went over the respirator settings and the blood gas results again, perhaps for the tenth time, and I recognized that there was nothing I could do for Jeremy at this time.

But I had two other patients: Mr. Cooper was visiting Mrs. Cooper and they were outside in the lobby. I felt I understood why they had responded in the way they had. There was no way they could fully accept the inert baby on the table as the son they had spent nine months hoping for, planning a lifetime for. They had never considered anything like this. They had seen their son flanked by machines, and he probably looked almost dead to them. The shock of the vision must have been enormous. If Jeremy lived, it would take time for the parents to come to know him. Two minutes in the nursery must have seemed an eternity. They probably were sitting there silently near their unknown son.

But in that visit a reality had been accomplished. They saw what I had said was true. And despite what could have been or should have been, they saw their son as he really was. The impact of the horror they had just witnessed would last; the reality was now more than words. The child was alive, and they felt thankful. But the tragedy of the years to come was not yet apparent to them, and they could not mourn because the life of their son had been saved. I saw that because of my own doubts and inability to change the situation, I was afraid to talk to the Coopers. I wished they had gone home.

I walked to the lobby and found them sitting in a corner, Mrs. Cooper in her dressing gown. I sat down without saying a word, sensing that they were happy I had come out to join them. I thought I knew a little of what they were thinking and my sadness extended out toward them.

"Is there anything I can do for you?" I asked, breaking the silence that had settled about us. Mrs. Cooper had been crying, but still looked strong and resolute in her conviction that her child would be well. There was no immediate answer to my question so I added, "I will be completely honest in answering any questions that you have."

They looked into my eyes, and I felt that a pact had been sealed. They accepted my offer. The promise to be honest is probably the hardest promise a physician can make because of the pain that sometimes comes with that honesty. Doctors can become artful in dodging painful questions, but I had made a commitment to the Coopers, and they had accepted that commitment. It was necessary for all of us to have someone to trust and share the grief. We had known each other for a very short while: I was the random doctor who was on call when the tragedy occurred, but now we were becoming closer than most relationships after ten years.

"Will he live?" Mrs. Cooper had wanted to ask the question in some other way, but she did not have the strength to put it more delicately.

"I do not know," I answered. "There are still many things that could possibly go wrong, but if he does well and learns to breathe without the respirator, I think he will live."

"Why did this happen?" she asked, beginning to cry again.

"I do not know," I answered.

"God will help you," Mr. Cooper said after the pause. After a few moments I explained that Dr. Carter (Emily) would be taking care of Jeremy during the night and that I would be back to see them in the morning.

"Dr. Carter will stop by later in the evening to tell you how Jeremy is doing," I said.

"Thank you," Mrs. Cooper whispered. They stood and started walking down the hallway to her room. It was feeding time and all the healthy babies were being brought out to their mothers for the five o'clock feeding. The Coopers would sit through feeding time silently.

(7)

The nursery seemed cold. It was about five in the afternoon and, perhaps because of my exhaustion, the rooms seemed dead, even with the machines efficiently humming and the nurses hurrying about to do their chores. The nursery had become an unhappy home, yet it was hard to leave it and go to some apartment where my clothes were kept.

No one was paying much attention to Jeremy. This often happened in the nursery with children like him. Babies who were recovering from a pneumonia would have nurses playing with them, giving them rattles, changing diapers, making mobiles over the cribs. But a child like Jeremy, a child who might die and whom some secretly hoped would die, received no love from the staff. Emily and Steve felt little for Jeremy; they had not talked with the parents, had not taken the responsibility for the decision to bring him back to life. Their emotional investment was in other infants. Steve was feeding Baby Boy Brown, a baby who was not gaining weight well. The nurses always kidded us about pediatricians not knowing how to feed a baby, so Steve was sitting in a rocking chair with a clean gown, trying to convince the stubborn baby to swallow a little delicious formula. But the baby acknowledged his efforts by promptly throwing up, and he carefully handed the child to a smiling nurse.

Jeremy's seizures were barely noticed. Every half hour a nurse would mark down the temperature, blood pressure, and pulse, but it was done without love. Of all the babies in the nursery, Jeremy was the least likely to find friends among the staff. He was a loser, and no one wanted to be around him whether he lived or died.

I asked Emily to be careful with Jeremy during the night, as a favor to me, and she understood what I meant. But a real part of me wanted to say, "If he dies during the night, then everything will be for the better." I could not consciously hope for my patient's death, but if he died, he died, and that would be that. He would be wrapped in a little white shroud and taken to the morgue and it would be over.

The only really difficult part of my job is managing the doubts, the ambiguities. I feel ambivalent when I see a healthy child born to a heroin addict, or when I see a child go home with parents who are known to abuse their children. With Jeremy there was ambivalence about wanting him to live. If he died, I could honestly say that I had done all I could for him. If he died, he would not have to go through life in the back wards of state hospitals. His parents would not have to endure the agony of never hearing their son learn to talk.

But what is this? What kind of a person am I who could wish that a life end? Am I a murderer because I see advantages in my patient's death? How can I be human? This is the richest nation on earth, and a good life must be possible for those not as healthy as others. And parents love their children, even those with serious medical problems. How can the thought that it might be better if Jeremy had died ever enter my head? But it did, and it does still, and I do not know the answers.

I know that I love life, that life is the most precious thing in the world, and to Jeremy, his life is just as precious as mine. But in unaltered nature, this child might now be dead, and the parents mourning a child they had never known. Am I right to try to alter the natural process?

Again Jeremy became two people: one, the bag of sand that would irrevocably change his parents' life, and two, the infant with curly black hair and gentle eyes whom I was coming to love.

(8)

After going home, saying hello to my wife, Karen, and eating dinner, I slept until the alarm rang at six o'clock the next morning. During the two conscious hours I had spent with Karen, she had been careful not to ask how the past two days had been; she could easily read it on my face. Also, we had promised never to talk about medicine, but I told her the story of Jeremy anyway.

It was my turn to buy doughnuts and coffee in the morning. I felt relaxed, perhaps a little tired, but I was eager to get back to work. Although disappointed that I would be missing a concert that evening, I was glad there were only seven more nights and fourteen more days of duty in the nursery. Then it was off to the emergency floor, which is considered the easiest rotation with lots of time off. Ah, but back to the nursery in two months.

Driving to work was nice—it was the only time I had to see the city. While other drivers were angry at the stop lights and traffic jams, I enjoyed them, knowing how terrible the next thirty-six hours would be. I thought of Jeremy often during the drive, wondering if he were still alive, if Emily had been able to take the tube out, what it would be like to talk with his parents again. My thoughts were distant. I was refreshed and my defenses were strong—Jeremy was just a case I was involved with yesterday.

My guilt was hidden, and I saw the decision to resuscitate Jeremy as obviously correct, for I could not have predicted the intracranial hemorrhage, and children who have been without air for fifteen minutes have done well without any damage. No other pediatrician I know would have done any differently. There had been no alternative. However, the defenses were not complete, and the question of whether life under any circumstances was better than death again entered my mind. But the drive to work was an opportunity to see this question in a completely different frame of mind. The slow, exhausted thinking was gone, and my mind wandered without emphasis over the thoughts that had pressured me the day before. The instant I entered the nursery, the pressure would return.

I changed from my street clothes into the scrub suits that we wear in the nursery, and I was on time. My first glance was toward Jeremy's heating table in the center of the room, and it was empty. My mind went blank until Steve told me that he had been moved over into the corner, and in the same breath asked for his coffee. The respirator was still going, so there couldn't have been much change. There were two new incubators in the room, so they had been busy.

"How was your night?" A standard question, but always important. I was asking about their state of mind rather than any of the details of the night. Fortunately, both Emily and Steve were mentally fit and I had little to worry about. They both thrived on this sort of work and were good at it. Each of us had slightly different styles, but we were all in it together.

"Not too bad," Steve replied. He was clean shaven and had just taken a shower. There were no new respirators going, so it couldn't have been that bad.

"What's over there?" I asked, pointing to the new incubators, sipping my coffee.

"Preemie twins, about two thousand grams each, and they're O.K." The babies were about four pounds each, so they wouldn't cause too many problems, I hoped.

"What about Jeremy?"

"Who?"

"Baby Boy Cooper . . . Jeremy . . ." I understood that his exhaustion and preoccupation with the two new infants had taken his mind off Jeremy.

"Oh, he did pretty well. We had him off the respirator for a couple of hours during the night, and he had only one apneic spell, but he came around quickly. Also, he's moving around a lot better, and maybe we can take out the tubes today." Steve re-recognized my interest in the baby and added, "We watched him carefully and moved him to the corner because he was doing well. We needed the space when the preemies came."

"How much sleep?" Another routine question as we ate through the pile of doughnuts. Emily came in after having been to the delivery floor to see if we were about to get any problems, and she was happy to see the coffee. Pam, of course, was late, and if she didn't arrive by seven-thirty, we would eat her doughnut. That threat was the only way we could get her to come in at all in the mornings. As usual, she showed up at seven twenty-five and drank the cold coffee and leisurely ate the doughnut. But she was never late on the mornings when she had to buy, because she understood what it was like to be without coffee.

"About three hours; I can't complain."

I was eager to start work rounds, where we go to each baby and discuss what has to be done during the day. Pam packed up her breakfast and brought it and the scut book along. Anything that had to be done would be listed in the scut book so we would not forget. We started in the observation nursery, where the infants were not critically sick. Emily ran the rounds, her last responsible act for the day, filling Pam and me in on what had happened during the night.

"Baby Miller gained two ounces, feeding well, send him downstairs," she said as we leafed through the chart on the side of his crib. Downstairs is the nursery for healthy children, and as we no longer considered Baby Miller sick, he graduated to the other floor. He had spent an easy two days in the observation nursery, as his reason for being there was that his mother had had an infection, and we wanted to make sure he did not have it also. This first promotion was celebrated by a brief note in the order book and a note in the scut book to call for the culture results.

The next baby we came to had some jaundice and was feeding poorly, so we decided to' check the level of jaundice and take some cultures, looking for an infection. Pam noted it down in the scut book.

We went through the next fifteen babies rather quickly as none seemed critical. But there were things to do, and the scut list grew. When we came to Jeremy's table, we saw a difference and, as Pam and I looked at the baby, we were optimistic. He was moving around, fighting the tube, opening his eyes more. He looked alive, almost trying to say, "Take this machine away, I can do it on my own." We looked at the charts where the blood gases, blood pressure, and other measurements were recorded, and all was in order; he had not had as many seizures as he had had yesterday. He was getting better, and we could hope that it would continue. Because of the improvement, we knew that the bleeding within his brain had stopped. Brain and nerve tissue that is destroyed can never be replaced, but tissue that is only mildly damaged can sometimes regain function. It would be years before we could know definitely how much permanent damage there would be, and although we still recognized that there might be extensive impairment, we were encouraged by the way he looked this morning. Perhaps, after all, he would grow up to be a playful, responsive child.

We discussed taking out the umbilical artery catheter because we no longer needed to do frequent blood gases. We would also take out the endotracheal tube from his airway and disconnect the respirator. If he stopped breathing, we would breathe for him by hand and then, if necessary, replace the tube. Jeremy would live, and although we kept him on the danger list, the worst seemed over in terms of life and death.

We saw the preemie twins and they looked well. They would need routine premature care and close watching, but their stay in the nursery would probably be quite easy for both them and us. We would feed them, and when they grew to be five pounds, they would go home. We then went downstairs to the regular nursery to see if any of those babies had become ill. Aside from minor matters, it looked like a good day coming up.

Work rounds over, we all began our chores. Emily and Steve started the scut list, drawing blood samples, filling out forms, calling for lab results. Pam went on "mother rounds," where she went to each mother and reported how her baby was doing. But she did not go to Mrs. Cooper. I would do that because I knew her better. Fortunately, Mrs. Cooper now had a separate room, so we would be able to talk openly about her baby.

I went upstairs and examined Jeremy closely. He was better, but no miracles had happened. All the signs of brain damage were still there. While he was moving about more and breathing better, his reflexes were still not normal, and his muscles were tight. But now he looked more like the baby that Mr. and Mrs. Cooper had been praying for.

When I said hello to Mrs. Cooper, she was eager for news. I explained the improvement and that we were going to take out the catheter and the endotracheal tube. I added that this did not mean he was out of danger, just that things were looking a little better. She had rested, and her hope was high that her prayers had been answered. She would come down to the nursery after ten and she could hold the baby.

It was easy to remove the umbilical artery catheter, and Pam did this as soon as I got back to the nursery. Over the umbilical cord we placed a simple clean bandage and the IV apparatus was removed. We then carefully removed

the tape around Jeremy's mouth which held the endotracheal tube and disconnected the respirator. Slowly we
pulled back on the tube and it slipped out from between
his vocal cords and out of his mouth. For the first time in
his life, he cried. We felt good, and standing beside him
for the next twenty minutes, we watched him breathe in
and out, crying hoarsely, coughing, moving around.

But then he stopped breathing; he had an apneic
spell. It was as if he forgot to breathe. He wasn't choking
or coughing; he just stopped breathing. His eyes were
open, but he lay still and began to turn blue. Pam placed
the oxygen mask over his face, and I slapped him on the
soles of his feet, and the breathing returned. Crying,
breathing, crying . . . steady, even breaths, about forty
per minute. Occasionally he would have a seizure which
would last about thirty seconds, but this didn't interrupt
his breathing.

We took away the respirator and brought over an
apnea monitor. This is a small machine that has a single
wire which is taped onto the chest and measures the
movement of the chest during respiration. If this movement should stop for fifteen seconds, an alarm sounds,
and we can then come over and help start the breathing
again. Because Jeremy was now free of the respirator and
catheter, he was free of the many problems that can be
caused by these aids, and we felt that his chances of living
were much better. Hopefully, in a day or two, he would
no longer even need the apnea monitor. But his breathing
would have to be perfectly normal, without a chance of
stopping.

With the machines removed, he looked more like a
normal baby, and because he no longer needed the warmer
table, we put him inside an incubator, the apnea monitor
wire coming out of the porthole. From across the room, he
looked like any other baby in the nursery.

Em and Steve were busy doing routine chores, and we
got a call from the delivery floor where a diabetic mother
was giving birth. We attend these births because of the

possible problems, but there was no emergency, and after the delivery I returned to the nursery. On the way I saw Mrs. Cooper, and together we went in to see her child. She, of course, saw the improvement and that there were none of the large machines surrounding her baby, but she was still frightened. I brought up a chair and a clean gown and, after she was seated comfortably, placed the infant on her lap, being sure that the single wire taped to his chest was not tangled. I felt it was important that she begin to know her child, even though he was still very sick, rather than continue to have this fear that would be hard to overcome later. Woodenly she held Jeremy, afraid to move, looking into his eyes. He had one ten-second apneic spell, but began breathing by himself before the monitor alarm went off, and his mother did not notice. I held my breath during those ten seconds. But what Mrs. Cooper saw was her son who had grown inside of her for nine months and who was now in her arms. It was like a short interview, but in time she would become less afraid and, I hoped, her love would grow.

The fragile infant was placed back into the incubator, and Mrs. Cooper left the nursery. She was welcome to come in at any time and would be able to feed her baby at the next feeding time.

The neurologist came over and examined Jeremy like a car enthusiast would examine a vintage Rolls-Royce. All the pathological signs were there. He said that this child, if he ever learned to breathe, would probably learn little else. A portable EEG (electro-encephalogram) machine was brought in and the eight wires were taped around Jeremy's head. This machine measures the electrical discharges of the brain and is a help in determining the amount of damage. The EEG showed very little functioning brain tissue—the worst news possible. The strangulation and the bleeding had destroyed almost all of Jeremy's brain. The neurologist wrote his note, thanking us for this interesting consultation, and left the nursery.

At visit rounds, little was said about Jeremy. We mentioned the EEG results and everyone nodded and said, "Well, we knew all along . . ." But I did not know it all along—I did not want to know it, and therefore I did not see it. But now it was on paper in front of me, and I could not deny it. Dr. Williams began to talk about the twin births and the management of preemies, but I could not listen. I was trying to imagine what it would be like for the Coopers for the next ten years.

Jeremy was a forgotten child in the corner. Whenever his alarm went off, which it did frequently, someone would go over and slap his feet to get his breathing started again. Otherwise people tried to stay away, as far away as possible. During my free time, I would stand beside his incubator. He was very special to me, and I am still not completely sure why.

In the afternoon a baby was transferred into the nursery from one of the smaller hospitals because of severe jaundice and anemia. Jeremy quickly became "yesterday's baby," no longer in the center of the room, no longer the center of my thoughts. As I worked on the new baby, only Jeremy's alarm was a reminder that he was still alive. He would stay in the nursery until he died or got better. I wanted to think about him, to get to know him, but I was soon too busy with other children. But whenever I heard it, I responded to his alarm.

(9)

The days pass quickly in the nursery, with new problems being discovered and treated, preemies gaining weight and going home, new sick children requiring our attention. But Jeremy's breathing did not improve.

He remained in the corner of the room, spending his time alone, his alarm signal reminding us of the enormous brain damage that was healing very slowly, if at all. He was fed regularly, his charts completed, but the miracle I was secretly hoping for had not occurred. Sometimes I would stand by his crib, just looking into his eyes, looking at his small hands. Other people would think that I was doing something medical, maybe examining him or counting his respirations, but I wasn't. I had stopped thinking about his future; I just saw him the way he was, a sleeping newborn, different from other infants. Jeremy had become an individual to me; he was no longer a bag of sand. And as the days passed I was getting to know him more and more. Occasionally, when it was quiet at night, I would pretend that I was a matronly nurse, put on a clean gown, and try to give him his formula. He would be wide awake, trying to suck on the nipple, which was difficult for him to do. The nurses would come around and give me pointers (they don't teach us these things in medical school), sometimes laughing at my inexperience. But they also recognized that I had developed a bond with the child, and my feeding him saved them time. Infants with brain damage are unable to suck well, and feeding consists of bending the nipple inside the mouth and forcing out the milk. I learned what his parents were learning, that he was not the normal child who would drink down a bottle of milk as soon as you put the nipple into his mouth. It would take an hour for Jeremy to swallow three ounces of formula. He did not cry like other children, and his arms and legs were very tight.

The neurologist came over every day to see Jeremy, and the medical students would examine all the reflexes, looking for the abnormal neurological signs, waiting for periods of apnea. One day the chief of neurology came to the nursery and lectured about brain damage, the physiologic mechanisms involved in the crossed extensor reflex, and why it was different in Jeremy. We learned from what he said and the medical students took notes. But this was Jeremy Cooper they were talking about, not some picture in a textbook.

In other respects he was doing fairly well. He was gaining weight, and there had been no new problems. His apneic spells always responded to a slap on the feet, and he had stopped having seizures. He was moving around more and sometimes seemed to look about the room. But there had been no miracles, and if he didn't learn to breathe, he would die, sooner or later. Jeremy was a "vegetable"; one of the neurologists called him a cabbage.

I felt a strong sense of responsibility toward both Jeremy and his parents, which Emily recognized. Whenever she saw something that had to be done, as a courtesy she would check with me before doing it. But aside from minor things, there was little to be done that could cause any improvement. His progress of the first two days had slowed down almost to a stop, and I could not pretend there was any chance of Jeremy's not being monstrously retarded. Instead, I saw that he could probably not even live outside of the nursery.

I saw the Coopers frequently during the days that

passed. They were more comfortable, taking Jeremy from his crib and feeding him the formula. They would play with him in the nursery, learning from his responses who he was. They were no longer afraid of him, and in the occasional times that he would stop breathing, they would rub his back or slap his feet until he started again. The Coopers at first had been pleased with his progress, but now they were growing more realistic about the damage that had been done. Yet there was hope—he looked almost like a normal baby, and I felt that they were growing to love him as he was, not just as they wished he had been. They noticed that the apneic spells were now less frequent, and that many times he would respond by himself.

But I was unable to share their hope that he would do well. His progress had almost stopped, and I saw that eventually an apneic spell would go unnoticed. It would be impossible for Jeremy to stay in the nursery his whole life, and at home in this condition he would eventually die. We talked about these things, and while they understood, they would also talk about wanting to take him home, once mentioning that they would buy him a football on his seventh birthday.

I said that I doubted if Jeremy would ever play football, I doubted that he would ever learn to walk. They nodded, accepting the reality briefly once again, and then began playing with their son. I liked the Coopers and I felt they liked me, but I was troubled that they did not share my pessimism. Yet I also recognized that their assumption that Jeremy would be a football-playing seven-year-old was an expression of their love. I did not know what would happen in the time to come, but the three of us saw Jeremy as an individual, a soul, perhaps different from other children, but nonetheless a person in his own right.

After about a week and a half, the staff sat down to discuss what should be done. As we sat in the comfortable chairs, I knew what Dr. Williams and John were going to suggest, and what we would agree to. The EEG's had been repeated and consistently showed almost no brain activity; the neurologist said that there was no hope of the infant's ever learning to do anything he was not able to do now; the damage was so severe, there was no chance for independent life. If the child were to go home, a parent would have to stand by his crib day and night to be sure that he kept breathing, and this was an intolerable burden to ask of any parent. He would die at home of an apneic spell eventually, or he would die of a pneumonia if he weren't carefully fed. The parents would be unable to spend one hour feeding him every four hours. A decision had to be made: should we continue as we were, or allow him to die quietly here in his crib? Should we disconnect the apnea monitor, and let him die if that was to be his future?

Because I knew the Coopers best, I discussed as accurately as I could what I felt they believed and wanted, saying that I thought they would accept any decision we were to make. I said that they were coming to know the problems involved with taking care of Jeremy and were preparing themselves for them. Those who wanted to withdraw "life support" argued that he would die anyway, and that it would be better now, so that the parents could forget and have other, more healthy, children. The discussion took a long time, and the vote was five to none in favor of withdrawing life support. We would no longer try to start his breathing if he should stop, but we would continue to feed him and give him routine care. He would have to breathe for himself or die.

This was the decision of the medical staff: Dr. Williams, John, Emily, Steve, and Pam. I abstained because, although I saw the reasons clearly, I could not agree to "kill" this child whom I was coming to love. Perhaps I felt that to vote against this was to say that I wanted to keep him alive and in the nursery indefinitely because I sort of liked him. I am a coward and I could not say that. But at the time I understood no reasons; I just could not agree with them, even though my vote had no significance.

I do not know what my decision would have been if it had been mine alone to make.

The agreement, of course, was dependent upon the understanding and consent of the Coopers. This was our medical advice, and I would talk to them and explain why we felt this way.

They came in later that afternoon, and we sat in the lobby. I explained as clearly as I could that we did not believe that Jeremy could live by himself, and that by keeping him alive we were just putting off the inevitable. If we removed the apnea monitor, he would stop breathing unnoticed, and if he were unable to start by himself he would die.

They agreed quite suddenly. In fact I sensed that they had been thinking about this and had independently decided to request it. "We believe that Jeremy will be cured," Mr. Cooper said. "We have been praying for him every day, and the time has now come to see God's will."

"We thank you," Mrs. Cooper broke in apologetically, "for all you have done, but you can do no more. You cannot cure him, only God can do that."

It was agreed. I did not mention my ambivalent feelings about the staff decision and was relieved that they wanted the same thing. They were seeking another specialist, and I wanted to wish them luck.

After the Coopers left for the day, the nurses were told not to resuscitate Jeremy, that if he stopped breathing to let him alone. A little sign was put on the side of his crib saying, "Jeremy Cooper—DNR." DNR means "Do Not Resuscitate." There was no talk of this in the nursery, for everyone accepted it as a reality, something that had to be done. The apnea monitor was disconnected and moved out of the room.

That night Pam and I were on duty. By the time Steve and Em went home, there had been no apneic spells that we had seen, and Jeremy looked the same in his crib. At first I didn't want to look over to that corner for fear of finding him dead. If someone else found him, then it would be all over. It was a quiet night, most of the routine work done. At times I would wander by Jeremy's crib, listening to his breathing, my mind with no thoughts.

At nine o'clock I looked through the window from the other room and saw that Jeremy was a pale gray. I walked over as slowly as I could, Pam noticing and walking over also. Jeremy was not breathing; his heartbeat was slowing down. There were two pediatricians standing next to a dying child doing nothing, just watching him die. His color turned to a darker gray, then to a deep blue color. During the one minute we watched, a billion conflicting thoughts raced silently through our minds. All the nurses had left the room and we were alone. It would be so easy to start him breathing again, just a slap on the foot; I was a murderer not to do it. I was watching Jeremy, a child whom I had come to love, die. I had accepted the staff decision not to resuscitate him, but I didn't mean for it to be like this. I wanted it to happen when I was at home, asleep.

I saw a lifetime of guilt ahead of me as I walked away from the crib. This is who I am, this is what I have done, and this is the life I have chosen. Pam called over—Jeremy had begun to breathe again, by himself. I looked and he was pink, his color returning, his breathing steady. He had not moved in his sleep. Confusion erased any emotion. Numb, I smoked my cigarette in the silence of the circumcision room.

(10)

During the night I did not sleep. It was quiet in the nursery, but the conflicts over Jeremy gave my mind no rest. He had one other apneic spell which I saw, and again recovered spontaneously after becoming blue. I knew now he was able to recover from these spells, but I did not know if he would every time. I was impatient for him to die—the staff had decided that he would and should die, but he was not doing it. He would recover after becoming blue, and perhaps he would continue to do so for the next ten years. He had not been listening to our decision.

Dawn came and the morning passed slowly. I was anxious, and when the Coopers came in at eleven, I was nervous about explaining what had happened during the night. They were dressed in their best clothes, carrying a Bible, and looked quite different than I had ever seen them before. The nursery gowns they put on looked like choir robes. As we walked over to Jeremy's crib they looked to the floor in silence as I began talking, nervously explaining that Jeremy had lived through the night. But they were not listening and seemed to be waiting for me to stop talking.

They had come to pray for their son.

Mrs. Cooper began in a slow monotone, saying, "Lord, please help Jeremy overcome this problem. He is Your soul, he is Your son. Please heal him and make his breathing good." As she continued without pausing, her voice became stronger and louder, the monotone slowly changing into a rhythmic chant. "The doctors have done all they can, Lord, and we are thankful to them, but it is now up to You. We know that You are able, You have the strength . . ."

Mr. Cooper simultaneously began praying, at first slowly, a rhythmic repetition of what his wife was saying. "Halleluiah, let the Lord heal . . ."

". . . that God should heal the sick, and make the crippled walk. Dear Lord, we ask only for life . . ."

"Halleluiah, let life come into Jeremy . . ."

"We know and believe in Your powers, we have felt of Your strength, halleluiah, to make our son whole . . ." The chants became a song, and their voices spread through the nursery. There were no other sounds, the nurses quietly slipping into the other room, and the song grew in its strength and beauty, the words pouring out spontaneously in the rhythm; no prepared prayers, but they sang their faith and fears to the God that was listening.

". . . let Jeremy grow to walk and talk, let him become one of Your children."

"You know that we believe, and Jeremy believes, halleluiah, please save his life, dear Lord, praised be Your name."

"Your name is sacred, and we thank all the human help, but we ask for You, God . . ."

The chanting and singing had reached a fever pitch, then slowly began to die away. The Coopers were pouring out their own words, in a rhythm and manner that only they could know, expressing with their faith and tears an emotion that I had never seen. As they spoke with God, they felt joy, in knowing that He would help, perhaps in the knowledge that they were doing all that they were able to; they had faith that Jeremy would be well. The words were becoming slow and solemn, as if they were exhausted by their prayers. They were no longer looking at their son, but ended the chants looking at the floor. I stared at Jeremy with tears in my eyes, not understanding a bit of what had happened.

As the Coopers looked toward the floor, Jeremy moved slightly, then stretched out his arms and opened his hands. For one second I thought I was watching the answer to their prayers. Then he stopped breathing. His chest did not move. I stood motionless, paralyzed, my eyes glued to his immobile chest, while the Coopers, still looking toward the floor, began to leave.

Mr. Cooper quietly apologized for making a commotion in the nursery and said he knew that we were busy. They did not see Jeremy becoming gray in color. I stared at the child. If they noticed, what should I do? Should I bring him back or let God answer their prayers? Before they noticed, Jeremy took a big breath and began to move about. The Coopers began to move toward the door, perhaps thinking that my silence had been a criticism of what they had done. We then said good-by warmly, and they left the nursery. I wondered if I had seen a miracle, but if it was, it was very confusing to me. God has never been very explicit with me, but then again, I have never spent much time listening to what He has said.

(11)

Over the next four or five days, Jeremy did fairly well. He was eating a little better and gaining weight. The periods of apnea had become less, and he seemed to be responding to them more quickly. Jeremy would probably live and even go home soon. I spent many long hours talking with the Coopers about the problems they would face over the years, and I introduced them to a program we had at the hospital for children like Jeremy.

The religious ceremony was never mentioned. I wanted to tell them that I thought it was the most beautiful thing I had ever seen parents do, how they had openly and honestly said what they wished and felt with the strength their religion has given them. But I never mentioned it because I was ashamed of my own ignorance. I did not have to tell them that their belief in God gave them strength.

I introduced the Coopers to Mrs. Simpson, in charge of the hospital program for brain-damaged infants. Her staff would help the Coopers in the months ahead with the enormous problems they would come up against, and help them adjust to the life they would have to lead. In this program Jeremy would have every opportunity to develop to his greatest capacity. Mrs. Simpson is a good, strong woman, able to talk with the Coopers in a way that I could not, as she has had years of experience dealing with situations exactly like this. The Coopers and Mrs. Simpson met once a day while Jeremy was in the hospital. Jeremy would go home, perhaps soon, and the parents would be given as much support as the staff could give.

My rotation in the nursery ended. I went to work on the accident floor while Jeremy was still in the nursery, and over the next week I would visit occasionally and talk with the Coopers, but my involvement began to taper off as I became immersed in other things. Jeremy continued to do fairly well, and one day when I came over, the new resident told me that Jeremy had been discharged and was now at home. The neurologists would see him every two weeks to look after his medical problems, and Mrs. Simpson began working with Jeremy and his parents in the clinic. I have never seen or heard from the Coopers since. I do not know if Jeremy is alive or dead. I am afraid to ask.

It is unfinished, and I feel hollow and empty. How could I not know the ending of a story about a child I had become so close to? I do not even know if an ending is possible. But I was on duty on the accident floor; I had to say good-by to the Coopers and take up new responsibilities.

If I had let Jeremy die that morning in the labor room, the parents by now would probably be starting to recover from their grief. But I didn't. With luck and special schooling . . . I do not know, I am afraid to think. Again the doubts and ambivalence do not allow me to see clearly what is before me. Perhaps the parents have learned a new life, different from the one they had been dreaming about. Perhaps they are in agony from seeing their maimed son. Perhaps they are mourning his death.

But the question is not resolved, and that is why, years later, I ask the same questions in a million different ways. If I really knew what the questions were, it would be easy to look up the Coopers and ask. But the greatest tragedy of ambivalence is that the exact nature of the questions is obscured.

part ii

Susan Jenkins

(1)

Our hospital, like so many city hospitals, was old and big, with long, rambling corridors—a subway system in the basement—and multicolored arrows pointing out the different stations in several languages. As I walked to the biochemistry lab with a tube of blood in my breast pocket, I took care not to bump into any of the filled garbage cans lining the walls, awaiting disposal. Over the past two years I had learned how to walk by the garbage cans so that my nursery robes would not brush against them and carry germs back to the children.

I was struck by the irony of our attempts to maintain cleanliness in the nursery by wearing white gowns over our scrub suits, then having to march through basement corridors infested with rats and cockroaches. It seemed ludicrous to think that a piece of cloth could keep off the dirt that had been accumulating in the tunnels for the past hundred years, but I guess it was better than nothing. The dirt, like the smell, seemed to hang in the air, and I would spend fifteen minutes washing when I returned to the nursery.

It had been a quiet night so far with only the seemingly endless routine scut work waiting to be done—a blood test here, a physical exam there. There were no critically ill patients, so we worked slowly and comfortably. The blood I had taken to the biochemistry laboratory belonged to Baby Boy Hernandez, who was jaundiced at eight hours of age, earlier than usual. Pam was writing in the charts, keeping up with the notes on each baby in the intensive care and observation nurseries. She wrote about Baby Hernandez: hematocrit—58; syphilis—negative; blood type—A positive; bilirubin—pending.

It had been Alice's birthday last week, and we all had chipped in and bought her a small jar of instant coffee. We had thought about getting a fancy coffee maker, but knowing how much she enjoyed stealing coffee from her friends in other parts of the hospital late at night, we decided just to get the instant coffee which she could keep for emergency use. Now she just had to steal hot water and sugar. There was always plenty of formula around to be used for cream.

We enjoyed a cup of coffee as Alice sang to the baby she was feeding. Alice said often that the reason she worked nights was because the nursing supervisor would not let her sing during the day. At night there was no one around to complain, and the babies liked it. We were waiting for the phone to ring, but it was quiet. Pam had just checked the delivery floor and there was no business for us. Even so, a quiet midnight and coffee meant that there was trouble ahead.

When the phone did ring I made no move, but relaxed as Alice began talking with her husband. He also worked nights and they enjoyed spending as much time on the phone as possible. Then the other phone rang, and when I answered it a voice said, "This is main emergency . . . we have a delivery coming in by ambulance."

The main emergency floor is about a quarter of a mile away from the nursery via the corridors in the basement. The doctors in main emergency know how to deliver babies but are nervous if the pediatricians are not there because of the risk of a sick baby. The chances of a bad baby are small, but greater than with a quiet, organized delivery on the delivery floor. Also, precipitous deliveries may mean small babies, so when a call like this comes in, we grab the emergency box and run to the accident floor.

Now, some Olympic sprinters can do the quarter-mile in forty-five seconds. But no one has ever broken the record set by Dr. Jim Cummins eight years ago when he ran the quarter-mile emergency ward sprint (stairs and corridors, with the emergency box and long flowing gown) in seventy-two seconds. But we tried. By the time we arrived at the emergency ward desk, several doctors were standing around waiting for the ambulance. They all seemed relieved that we had arrived, but we were so out of breath we couldn't see straight. I sat on a bench with two patients as the sirens grew louder.

When the stretcher came through the emergency doors, I saw that the baby had not yet delivered, and I started setting up our equipment in the surgical room. The obstetrician asked the mother some questions as ne washed and put on sterile gloves, and nurses and medical students lifted her onto the table. She seemed young and frightened, perhaps twenty, and no family had followed the ambulance to the hospital. Between contractions she would look to the corners of the room without expression, as if to deny her fear and loneliness.

Pam took a sterile towel and stood waiting to receive the infant. I introduced myself and took her hand as she screamed and pushed. The baby's head appeared, then the face. After the shoulders delivered, the infant's body quickly came out. The child gasped, slowly beginning to move about, then, as the cord was cut, began to cry. The obstetrician handed the squirming infant to Pam, who carried the child to the waiting incubator. I did not move, as I could see from across the room that the child was about seven pounds and there would be no emergency.

"You have a baby girl, Mrs. . . . Mrs. Jenkins," I said, reading her name off a piece of paper that had been brought in. "She looks fine."

Mrs. Jenkins, now breathing deeply, stared up at the ceiling with a look of exhaustion and confusion. She said nothing and closed her eyes.

"Do you want to see your daughter?" I asked after a pause.

"No . . . not right now. I will see her later," she said, grimacing as the obstetrician began to deliver the placenta. I went over to the incubator, and Pam said that everything was fine. We dried off the child and, with a bulb syringe, sucked some of the mucus out of her mouth. She had a strong clear cry and a nice pink color. We brought the incubator over toward Mrs. Jenkins.

"Would you like to see your daughter or should we take her to the nursery?" I asked hesitantly, confused by the blank expression on Mrs. Jenkins' face.

"Take her up to the nursery. I will see her later," she answered.

"All right. She will be in the observation nursery, and whenever you want to see her just tell the nurses." She continued to stare at the ceiling as we left, rolling the portable incubator out of the surgical room.

We labeled a tube of placental blood with the baby's name and left it at the emergency ward desk to be sent to biochemistry. Slowly we wound our way through the corridors toward the nursery with Baby Girl Jenkins, hoping that the plastic hood of the incubator would keep out the dark, damp basement air.

(2)

Some mothers don't want to see their babies right after childbirth. At first I was surprised at this, wondering why, after so much pain, a mother would not want to see the product of her labor. But it happens, and Pam and I did not think much about it as we walked back toward the nursery with the infant. At this time of night we tried to think about as little as possible.

We brought the incubator to the observation nursery because the baby was "dirty." There had not been time for the usual preparations, and Mrs. Jenkins had not even been washed before the baby was born. Childbirth in the hospital is performed under sterile conditions in an attempt to cut down the possibilities of infection. The mother is shaved and draped with sterile towels, and the obstetrician is gowned and gloved like a surgeon. But Baby Girl Jenkins was born on a table in the emergency floor, thus making her a dirty baby. Babies born in a dirty environment run a higher risk of infection, and for that reason we would take cultures and watch carefully. If she started to look sick, we would take more cultures and begin treatment with antibiotics.

But Baby Girl Jenkins was not a worry. Usually, in situations like this, after three days of uneventful observation the healthy child goes home with mother and there are no problems. Yet, because Mrs. Jenkins had not had prenatal care, we would run a few tests on the baby, among which would be tests for blood type and syphilis. I was always amazed that some mothers did not have prenatal care, even though it could be found free of charge or through welfare. I made a mental note to ask Mrs. Jenkins about this on mother rounds the next morning. Pam and I talked briefly about what we would do for the baby, and then, after examining her, I washed my hands carefully, afraid of carrying some disastrous bacterial infection to the rest of the infants. With some white adhesive tape on the floor, we marked off the corner of the room where Baby Jenkins would stay so everyone would be alerted that she was a dirty baby. If you wanted to step over the tape to hold Baby Jenkins, you had to wash your hands, put on a special gown, then carefully wash afterward. In a sense, everyone in the nursery was afraid of this new baby because she might be carrying an infection, and I wondered if the child would somehow recognize that people were avoiding her in this taped-off area.

Pam put on a sterile gown, washed up again, and examined our new admission, talking to her as she went along. "O.K., now, take a deep breath please . . ." And the baby would breathe in while Pam held the stethoscope to her chest. People sometimes think it strange that we talk to our patients the way we do, but it is not really all that different from the way some doctors talk with their adult patients. And the answers that adults give are sometimes no more helpful than the grunts of our patients. Pam told Baby Girl Jenkins that she was going to have a quiet stay in our nursery and that she was not to cause us any trouble, thank you. But the baby was not listening and began to suck on her knuckles. At this age babies have a hard time finding a thumb to suck on, so the whole hand goes into the mouth.

While Pam was examining Baby Jenkins, I sat in the nurses' station, smoking a cigarette, talking to Alice, and writing orders for the new admission. There was no

thought put into writing orders—they were habit, as rote
as signing your name:

1. adm obs n
2. dx-out of asepsis
3. cond-gd
4. vs q 4hrs
5. NPO q 4hrs
6. D5W q 4hrs x 2 as tol
7. form q 4hrs as tol
8. skin mouth vernix cult
9. wt q d
10. priv
11. adm bath
12. cord care

Medicine, of course, has its jargon, and doctors sometimes
smile proudly when they realize that people outside of
medicine are unable to understand what is being said.
Roughly translated, my orders were:

1. admit to the observation nursery
2. diagnosis—dirty baby
3. condition—good
4. vital signs (temperature, pulse, respiratory rate) every
   four hours
5. nothing to eat or drink first four hours
6. sugar water every four hours twice, as tolerated
7. formula every four hours thereafter, as tolerated
8. culture of skin, mouth and vernix
9. daily weight
10. mother may visit as desired
11. bathe in sterile water on admission
12. routine care of umbilical cord

This jargon is certainly no more distinguished than the
lingo that accumulates in any profession, something that
is easily understood by those who work with it all the time,
yet not often understandable to those outside of the pro-

fession. This medical language, or "medicalese," is something that house officers pride themselves on. It is a mark of status to be sufficiently fluent to say six or more complete sentences without a single intelligible word. These medicalese sentences are often said in such a way that the listener is completely confused and imagines the speaker to be very smart because he seems to know what he is talking about. During visit rounds we practice our medicalese with John and Dr. Williams, who over the years have become quite expert.

It stayed quiet, and at about two in the morning we went to the call rooms and fell asleep instantly. The delivery floor was empty, and there were no babies who were critically sick, so I enjoyed the luxury of taking my shoes and stethoscope off.

Four hours later the phone rang, and I became awake instantly. As I reached for the phone, I also reached for my stethoscope, my feet groping along the floor looking for my shoes. "Hello," I said to the phone.

"Hello, Doctor, I'm sorry to wake you up," said the voice, and I relaxed and almost stopped listening. Any call that starts off like that was not an emergency call. "Baby Jenkins just had a large loose watery stool after her first feeding."

"What time is it?" I asked.

"Six-thirty."

"O.K., I'll be out in a few minutes." I hung up the phone, yawning. It had been a good night, four hours of sleep. I would not complain, for it meant that I would be able to enjoy the night off instead of having to make up sleep. Diarrhea in Baby Jenkins—it could be the first sign of an infection or it could be nothing. I got up and went over to the sink to brush my teeth.

Baby Girl Jenkins looked well. She was active, and pink, moving about and looking around. Her cry was strong, perhaps a little shrill, but she didn't look like an infected baby. She had had one loose bowel movement which we cultured, but she did not look sick; I decided to wait and see what would happen. Steve and Emily came in at seven and we sat enjoying coffee, talking about many things, but not the nursery. It was a relaxed morning; we made our work rounds very slowly.

The delivery floor called and left a message that an elective Caesarian section would be starting in ten minutes, so Pam went up for the delivery. The mother had had several previous C-sections, and there was no suspicion that the baby would be sick for this one, but one of us always went up for a C-section. I would go on mother rounds while Emily and Steve began work on some of the problem babies.

Mother rounds are always a challenge. About 95 percent of our time was spent with the sick babies, and we knew little or nothing about the healthy ones. But 90 percent of the mothers on the maternity wards had healthy babies. We would go to each mother carrying a clipboard with charts that the nurses had filled out with each baby's age, weight, and sex, and, pretending that we knew the infants well, would ask the mother if she had any questions about her baby. Because we had no idea of what the healthy babies even looked like, it was hoped that no questions would be asked. We would even unconsciously develop the technique of asking if there were any questions in such a way that the mother would always say "No" whether she had questions or not.

When I came into Mrs. Jenkins' room I was relieved because I knew her baby. "How are you this morning?" I asked.

"I'm fine, thank you." She did not look at me and there was an edge in her voice.

"Have you seen your daughter yet?"

"I have no daughter. I want to give her up for adoption." As she said it she turned away and began looking for a cigarette.

"Why?" I asked after a pause.

"I don't want any more children."

(3)

It became clear why she had not wanted to look at her daughter the night before. Perhaps she had not decided completely, but she did not want to see the infant's face and grow attached to it. She was now trying to forget the child, to make believe that it did not exist. As I talked with her, I learned the reason for some of the anger that she held toward the child, the hospital and the doctors, and toward herself for not wanting the child. I saw a tiny part of the enormous complexity of her life: no husband, one other demanding child, and no money to support them other than inadequate city aid. Her apartment building was falling down, and there was plywood nailed across the first-floor windows to keep the vandals out. In five minutes I was overwhelmed by these problems that I could do little about. She wanted to give her daughter up for adoption; in her mind she saw it as the only way that her daughter would have a chance in life.

As she talked, releasing stored feelings, hidden perhaps for years, I sat looking at the floor, saddened by her loneliness, feeling guilty about the comforts of my own life. For whatever reasons, she had been abandoned by society, trapped in an endless circle of poverty. She talked with a mixture of anger and resignation; there was nothing to bring her child home to except the rats who fed on the loneliness of her empty life.

This was her hospital, and in many ways it reflected

her life. The first rat I ever saw was in the basement corridors of the hospital, but for Mrs. Jenkins, rats were constant neighbors. It was possible that her daughter, if given up for adoption, would not grow up living in a decayed apartment building that had only occasional heat, or with a bitter, angry mother who could not fight back because of the children she had to take care of. But the only way was for Mrs. Jenkins to give up her new child and never see or hear her again.

As I sat and listened, I felt my own anger rise—anger toward a society where such extremes could live in silence beside one another, anger toward myself for having an education paid for by my ancestors' money. I would never have to live in an apartment like that even if I had no money, but Mrs. Jenkins could not be heard, she had no social power. She could only sit at home and watch her children pull plaster from the bathroom walls. I was uncomfortable and wanted to leave.

"Have you spoken to the social worker about this yet?" I asked.

"No, I haven't. I just decided to give her up for sure a little while ago. I am sorry if I have taken up your time." Although she was young, perhaps twenty, she looked quite old and defeated. She had taken a shower, but the worry on her face had not passed as quickly as the childbirth six hours earlier. I was embarrassed that she had so quickly recognized my impatience and assumed that I was angry at her. I wanted to tell her that I felt sorry for her, that I was angry at the world for not giving her a choice, that I was angry at myself for wanting to get away from her. But I did not know how to say it. She had probably seen rejection so many times that she was not surprised by mine.

"I will tell Mary Allison, the social worker, and she will try to help. She will give you some forms to fill out and papers to sign for the adoption, and maybe she can help you find some new housing and day care for your child. If that were possible, do you think you could go out and find a job?"

I think she recognized that I was not doubting her but asking only out of curiosity. "I don't know," she answered.

"I will not be talking with you any more because I will be taking care of the child. Usually, once a mother makes the decision not to keep her child, she would rather not see the child's doctor. But I would like to try to help, and I will talk to Mary Allison about it."

"All right." She was looking toward the floor. It was done; she had decided to give up the child and had told me about it. I sensed that this was a turning point in her life, either an admission that life was too much for her, or that she was going to start to fight back. Either way, I think she felt that she had to be free of this new infant because of the danger ahead. It would be the safest thing for the child. Perhaps someone rich from the suburbs would adopt her and she would grow up without knowing the kind of unhappiness her real mother had known. Perhaps, but Mrs. Jenkins would never know, only hoping for a brighter future for her unknown daughter.

"I hope that things work out well for you," I said. Our communication, however brief, had been pertinent, and her confession to me that she did not want the child had been difficult for her to make. I wished that I had been able to do something, but I knew the best thing I could do was to leave and not return. I hoped that Mary would be able to help.

"Thank you," she said, still looking toward the floor. "Good-by." I turned and slowly walked out of the room.

The rest of mother rounds went quite quickly, the only incident being when I misread Baby Osborne's weight as six pounds, eight ounces instead of eight pounds, six ounces. Mrs. Osborne asked me if her baby really had lost two pounds.

Mary's office was at the end of the hallway on the maternity floor and was a nice place to visit. There were comfortable chairs, a coffeepot, plants growing on the windowsill, and it was always nice to talk with Mary. Because this had to do with patient care, I did not feel that I was wasting time; I could justify my spending fifteen minutes drinking coffee in her office. Mary smiled as I came in.

"What is it today?" she asked. "I haven't even finished the last terrible case you gave me."

"What makes you think I have another bad case for you? Maybe I just want a cup of coffee," I said, stirring in the sugar.

"No . . . it's another bad case, I can tell."

"No," I fought back, "it's not a bad case. It's rather a simple one, just an adoption." I didn't want to tell it all at once because then I would not have an excuse to sit and relax and finish my coffee leisurely. And this was a simple case, just some adoption forms and a check with the Housing Authority, that's all. "How's the baby market?"

"Booming. White or black?"

"White female."

"No problem. The waiting list is almost two years. Is she healthy?" Mary looked at me suspiciously.

"Yes."

"How many fingers?"

"She has all ten, I think. . . . Really, there's nothing wrong with her," I insisted. But Mary was always worried that there was something more, and there usually turned out to be more. Somehow even simple cases turned complicated when Mary got involved. We talked for ten minutes about the baby, and Mary wrote down Mrs. Jenkins' name and room number. As I turned to leave I thanked her for the coffee. "But . . ."

"I knew it."

". . . well, maybe you could look into the housing situation. She lives in the Elmwood Street Project and it sounds terrible. Anyway, maybe you could talk to her."

"That's an awful project," Mary said. "But there isn't much other housing around. Nothing else?"

"I hope not: She seems to be having enough trouble the way it is." I thanked her for the coffee.

"It's nothing. I enjoy supplying everyone in the hospital with my coffee," she said, smiling. "Someday I'm going to put some Ex-Lax in it and you'll be sorry." Mary's humor, like most hospital humor, tended to be a little earthy.

In the nursery Pam was with the new admission, the baby born by C-section. There had been no problems, and the baby was well. I told her about Baby Girl Jenkins as we began clearing up the rest of the scut work.

(4)

By early afternoon the nursery had become busy again. Emily and Steve were with a transfer from another hospital, and Pam was at x-ray doing an IVP on a baby with large kidneys. Baby Girl Jenkins had another diarrheal stool, and when I went over to look at her, she looked sick. It is hard to describe what it was that made her look sick to me; it was just a feeling. Something was very wrong. Diarrhea in a newborn is always dangerous because of the risk of dehydration, but she had had only two stools so far. Her color did not look as good as it had before, and she was "nervous," and seemed to have an anxious look on her face. The tone of her muscles was slightly increased, and she was a bit jaundiced. Worst of all, she had a temperature of 100.2. There was no one sign that was all that bad, but all these small signs together in a baby who was in a taped-in area of the nursery made me very worried.

It was not an emergency, yet I did not want to waste any time in getting started. There was an infection someplace; she was a "setup" for infection, and now she was showing the early signs. I did not know where, but the important thing was to do all the tests quickly and begin the antibiotics. Speed was important now. Working slowly, doing all the tests could take a couple of hours, and with some infections, that would be too long to wait. If she had meningitis, for example, she could be dead in two hours.

The intravenous was first. If the baby was going to have a lot of diarrhea, we would have to give large amounts of fluid by vein. Because the best veins in a baby are in the scalp, I took a razor and shaved off a little patch of hair and inserted an intravenous needle into a vein there. If Mrs. Jenkins had not given the child up for adoption, I certainly would have told her about this first, for shaving hair off a baby's head is just about the worst thing that can be done to an infant from a mother's point of view.

With the IV in place and taped securely, I made a small cut on the heel and filled up five tubes of blood for a bilirubin, blood calcium, and blood glucose level. Jaundice is common in all newborns, but coming before twenty-four hours of age, and with the other symptoms, it suggested infection. If the bilirubin test were very high, this would be even more suggestive. Another sample of blood was drawn under sterile conditions for a blood culture, to see if there were bacteria in the blood. As I worked, the infant began to look worse. She had a gray-yellow tinge to her skin, and she was jittery. The anxious look on her face occasionally changed to one of panic—desperate and sick. I clapped my hands loudly near her ear and she jumped and began trembling, her cry loud and harsh.

My fear was mirrored by the look in her eyes, and I began to work rapidly so I could begin the antibiotics. Cultures of urine and spinal fluid had to be taken before starting the drugs or else the cultures might be useless, and we would never know where the infection was located. I could not wait for the baby to urinate, so I pushed a long needle through her abdominal wall and into her bladder, drawing out a sample of urine for culture. I pulled the needle out, rolled her on her side, and began to prepare for the spinal tap, which I hoped would be just as easy. The needle passed through the space between the vertebrae and entered into the fluid of the spinal canal, the clear fluid running through the small tubing and into the test tube I held in my hand.

With the tap finished and all the cultures collected, I took a syringe filled with antibiotic and injected it into the vein on her head, through the IV. I was treating blindly. I had no idea where the infection could be, so I was treating for the worst, supposing the infection to be in the blood or the brain. Because the cultures would take two days to tell us the answer for sure, I had to guess which kind of bacteria it was likely to be, and choose antibiotics that I hoped would work. If this were an unusual kind of infection and I had chosen the wrong antibiotics, the baby could die.

The baby's first symptom had been diarrhea, which could be present with any infection but was suggestive of a bowel or urine infection. But the symptoms told us only that she was very sick, not what was causing the illness or where, specifically, it was located. We would now have to wait for the culture results.

After sending the cultures to the bacteriology laboratory, I still had to look at the fluids under the microscope. But I could slow down now, as the antibiotics were started. The specimens might give us a hint of where the infection was, but I doubted it.

I was about to leave for the lab when a nurse from the maternity floor came in and said that Mrs. Jenkins had just signed out of the hospital AMA. Signing out "AMA" means signing out "Against Medical Advice" and does not refer to the medical political organization. But the letters are an ironic coincidence.

I stood motionless for a moment, putting together the clues that lay before me. The mother was leaving the hospital, something that happens often when the child is being put up for adoption, because it is often difficult for her to be near her child. But there were other reasons why people signed out AMA. I ran down to the maternity floors and into Mrs. Jenkins' room. It was empty. At the desk I was told that she had just taken the elevator down, so I ran down the stairs and caught her just outside the front doors of the hospital as she waited for a bus.

"Hello, Mrs. Jenkins," I said, out of breath. "Can I speak with you for a minute?" I felt ridiculous standing at the bus stop in my nursery gown.

"What do you want?" she asked coldly. There was an edge to her voice, and I thought that I knew what I wanted to find out.

"Mrs. Jenkins, are you a heroin addict? I have to know for the baby's sake." There was no one else around who could have heard.

"No . . . why?" She was nervous and jumpy; she was starting to withdraw and had to leave the hospital to go home and get another shot. And the baby was going through withdrawal also.

"The baby is sick and has all the signs of heroin withdrawal. I can help the child more if you tell me whether or not you use heroin." After a pause I added, "Please don't be afraid. I have to know for the baby's sake."

But she could say nothing, and I could see that I had been right. No words would come out of her mouth. She started to cry and, looking at me, rolled up her sleeve, revealing thick scars over some of the veins. "Will the baby be all right?"

"I think so."

We nodded to each other and I walked back to the nursery. The diagnosis was made; the child did not have an infection but was withdrawing from heroin.

(5)

I walked back to the nursery slowly, chagrined that I had not thought about addiction before. The presenting symptoms of infection and heroin withdrawal are the same, but the tape on the floor around her crib kept yelling "Infection" into my ear. Withdrawal never once entered my mind. Now it was all clear. Mrs. Jenkins waited until the last possible moment before coming to the hospital because she did not want to withdraw: the baby was born on the accident floor. It had been in such a hurry that Mrs. Jenkins still had her sweater on when the baby was born and no one saw the needle marks. And she signed out of the hospital as soon as she began to withdraw.

The baby probably would be all right. Heroin withdrawal still has a high mortality rate, but it was better than a blood or brain infection. When a mother is a heroin addict, the baby is addicted while still in the womb. At the time of birth there is no more of the narcotic, and about six or eight hours later the baby begins to withdraw, going through almost the same torture that the adult would have to go through: diarrhea, fever, cramps, nervousness, sometimes even seizures. We would treat this by giving either paregoric, a narcotic that would replace the heroin, or a tranquilizer to make the withdrawal symptoms less severe.

Inside the nursery I went over to Baby Girl Jenkins' crib and looked at her. She was shaking and yawning, obvi-

ous signs of heroin withdrawal. I had been blinded to the
yawning before because it didn't go along with an infection. But I could see it clearly now. Because there was still
a remote possibility of there being an infection present, I
would continue the antibiotics at least until we had the
result of the cultures. I wrote an order for paregoric in the
order book, then took the urine and spinal fluid to the
lab to look at them under the microscope.

Emily and Steven also seemed to be getting busier
and busier during the day, as they worked with John on
the new transfer baby who had a congenital heart defect.
After writing a long note in Baby Jenkins' chart, I went
downstairs to discharge some of the healthy infants. I had
a feeling that when Alice came into the nursery tonight
Baby Jenkins would get a name, perhaps because she
would be with us in the nursery for the next month or so.
We could not discharge her until she was adoptable, and
that meant that she had to be completely withdrawn from
heroin. And if she were going to be here a month she
needed a name. . . . Junkie Jenkins? As I did the physical exams, my mind ran over a few names, but Alice was
the only one who could name the children.

By about four in the afternoon I went upstairs and
saw Baby Girl Jenkins again. She was a little quieter, her
color slightly improved, but she still looked sick. Somehow
knowing that she was withdrawing from heroin rather than
having an infection made her look better to me. But I felt
sorry for her, crying, shaking, sweating. . . . I wondered
if she was questioning why she had ever come into this
frightful world.

The phone rang and it was for me. "Doctor, I want
to take my baby home," Mrs. Jenkins said.

"Why?" I asked. "Why have you changed your mind?"

"Because she is my baby and I want to take her
home," she answered.

We talked briefly on the phone, and I told her that
the baby was sick from the heroin withdrawal, and would
be very sick over the next week or more, and could not

possibly go home before then. We would need to talk about this, and she agreed to come in and talk with Mary and me in the morning. As I hung up the phone, I sank back into the chair and sat motionless for about ten minutes.

I walked down the hall to Mary's office reluctantly because I had promised her that this was going to be an easy case.

"Hi," I said to Mary as I came into the room.

"Hi. What is it now?" Mary likes me but is afraid of the cases I bring in.

"It's about that baby I told you about this morning, the baby up for adoption," I said a little nervously.

"I knew it," she said. "I knew there was no such thing as a simple old adoption. I knew it wasn't going to be simple when I first saw you this morning. Well, tell me about it very slowly—I couldn't handle it all at once."

"Well," I started out slowly, "Baby Jenkins is sick and seems to be withdrawing from heroin, and Mrs. Jenkins just called me and wants to take the baby home with her."

Mary moaned and began to write something on her pad. Looking up, she asked, "You are telling me the truth, aren't you?"

I nodded. "Mrs. Jenkins will be coming in at ten tomorrow morning to talk with us." I got up to leave. "I'm sorry."

"The worst," Mary said, doodling on her pad. "A social worker's nightmare. Why do you do this to me?"

"Because you are the only person in the city who could begin to do a good job on a case like this." I was being honest.

(6)

At ten-thirty Mrs. Jenkins knocked on the outside door of the nursery. She was shown in by one of the nurses after she had washed and put on a clean gown. I met her in front of her daughter's crib, standing in the corner of the room still marked off with the white tape on the floor. "Good morning, Mrs. Jenkins," I said.

"Hello. How is she doing?" She stared for the first time at her daughter, seeing immediately that something was wrong. The baby was still in florid withdrawal, and the expression on the child's face was strained and anxious, a sharp contrast to the sleeping "contented" infants in nearby cribs. The baby was trembling all over, sucking her fist for relief when the pacifier fell out of her mouth. With any noise she jumped, as if shocked, and began crying with a harsh, piercing cry that would lead to a pathetic facial expression. "I know just how she feels," Mrs. Jenkins said.

"She is doing a little better this morning," I said. "We are giving her paregoric, a narcotic, to help her through the withdrawal."

"Can I hold her?" she asked hesitantly as the infant cried.

"Yes, of course." The baby did not quiet down when she was picked up but seemed to cry louder, the same as when the nurses would pick her up. With this much pain, being held was not comfort enough. I wondered whether, twenty years from now, Baby Girl Jenkins would still be suffering because of this rude entrance into life.

"Her name is Susan." The tone of Mrs. Jenkins' voice almost implied a question—as if she were asking if she were allowed to name her daughter.

"Hello, Susan," I said to the infant.

I went into the other room and lit up a cigarette, to let Mrs. Jenkins be alone with her daughter. I was worried about the outcome, whatever it was to be, but I felt it was important that they be alone for a while. I smoked slowly and after a little while went back in and suggested that we go to Mary Allison's office for our talk.

Mary had met Mrs. Jenkins the morning before when she had taken in the adoption forms to be signed. When we walked in, Mary asked us to help ourselves to coffee. Mrs. Jenkins began talking.

"I have changed my mind about giving my baby up for adoption. She is my baby, and I want to take her home." She seemed defensive and at the same time a little astonished at her own forcefulness. I sat down in a chair in the corner of the room.

"Well," Mary began, "there are a few things that I think we should discuss first."

"Because I signed those papers yesterday?"

"No, that is not a problem. Mrs. Jenkins, how much heroin do you use a day?" Mary looked into her eyes.

There was a pause, then, "Six bags."

"How do you support the habit?"

"A friend . . . the baby's father helps me." She looked at Mary as she answered and her voice was low.

"Do you think that you will be a good mother for the child?"

Mrs. Jenkins paused and then began crying softly. She had wanted to say "Yes" quickly, but her own doubt had stopped her. After a while she answered, "I think so."

The ice was broken; they were no longer two strangers sitting across the desk from one another, forced to talk. The conversation became less strained as they discussed the details of Mrs. Jenkins' life at home. Mary's direct questions about the drug use and the personal problems troubling Mrs. Jenkins seemed to be answered honestly. Mrs. Jenkins had been using heroin steadily for about eight months now, and she said that she wanted to quit.

"Enough to get into a heroin treatment program and stay with it?" Mary asked.

"I think so."

"Our concern is for Susan's safety," Mary began slowly. "Sometimes children of addicted parents get into a lot of trouble." There was an unusual tone in Mary's voice as she paused. "Do you know what kind of trouble I mean?"

Mrs. Jenkins looked up with an anxious glance and was silent.

Mary reached into the top drawer of her desk and brought out a hospital record. "You have a son named William, don't you?"

"Yes . . ."

"Could you tell us exactly why he was admitted to the hospital four months ago?"

My heart sank, for there was only one thing that Mary could be getting around to. Mrs. Jenkins said that Billy fell off the bed.

"I don't believe that he could have gotten two broken bones falling from a bed two feet off the floor. Also, we have pictures showing strap marks across his back. Did you beat your son?" Mary's cross-examination was met with a cold stare.

"No, I did not hit him. I was out . . ." Her voice trailed off as she realized she had just admitted that her son had been beaten.

"Go on," Mary urged.

"I was out and Sam beat him . . . we had been fighting, and I left the house for about an hour, and when I came back, I found him in the crib like that. I didn't hit him, ever." She began crying softly and there was silence in the room. I went over and picked up the chart and looked through it. It was apparent that there had never been any doubt about child abuse, but the child had not been taken out of the family because there had been no other proof and the case would have been lost in court. Both bones in the right forearm had been broken, and there were welts and strap marks across the child's stomach and back. I felt very sad, sad that anyone could possibly beat a child this way.

For the next half hour Mrs. Jenkins explained in detail what was going on in her life now. She had not seen Sam for three months, and her mother was helping out with Billy. She said that she wanted to give up heroin and make a fresh start.

"Well, we have been talking for quite a while," Mary broke in. "What do you think we should do?" She looked at Mrs. Jenkins and waited for an answer.

"I don't know," she said, crying. She had not expected Mary to have known about Billy.

"I have to be honest with you," Mary said. "You have two strikes against you. If we feel that Susan's life is in danger if she goes home with you, then we will have to try to prevent it through the courts and send Susan home with foster parents. But you say that you want to change, and there is time for you to show us that you are able to change. Susan will have to stay in the hospital for about a month to completely withdraw from heroin. That will give us time to get to know each other better, perhaps get you started in a heroin treatment program, and for you to decide what will be the best thing for your daughter. If you love her enough, you will prepare yourself to take good care of her."

There was a pause and Mrs. Jenkins looked toward the floor. "What does that mean?" she asked.

"It means several things. First, as long as she is in the hospital you will come in and feed her, get to know her. It also means that your children don't get any more broken bones." There was a long silence. "Anyway, that's enough for today. I am sorry that I have been so blunt, but I had to be honest about where things stand. You have the choice now, and it is a difficult choice to make. It means hard changes, and whether or not you want to change is something that only you know, deep inside. But think it over carefully, and we will talk again tomorrow."

"All right," Mrs. Jenkins replied. As she stood up, she looked very old and tired. But I sensed that she had seen that there was no alternative but to change, not just because of what Mary had said, but because she could not be happy leading the life she was leading now.

"About ten in the morning, right here . . ." Mary held the door open and shook Mrs. Jenkins' hand. I nodded good-by.

Mary shut the door, then slumped down in the armchair. "What do you think?"

I knew what Mary's decision had been, and she knew that I agreed with it: that we would give Mrs. Jenkins every chance possible and hope that things turned out well. "I guess this is the best thing," I said.

"Why can't people lead nice, simple, quiet lives?"

"It would be so boring," I said. "Besides, you'd be out of a job."

(7)

I felt uneasy for the rest of the day. Mary and I had made a decision about Susan Jenkins and it was the kind of decision that I suspected would be wrong either way. I guessed that the chances of its working out perfectly would be roughly one in a million. But I wasn't hoping for perfection. I hoped only that Susan would grow up in a stable, loving home. Like most of medicine, this solution was a compromise. Unfortunately, there were no numbers that we could feed into a Terrible Tillie to get an answer. We were guessing on probabilities and our own biased view of human nature. And if we were wrong, Susan could die.

There is no place to seek advice in situations like this. If I wanted to get advice on the best drug to use in heroin withdrawal, I could call ten different neonatologists and get their opinions. But not here. I asked John, and his advice was as good as any. "There are no set answers. It all depends upon the people involved."

The risks involved in sending Susan home were great. Even if Mrs. Jenkins herself had not beaten Billy, he had been beaten at home and his arm had been broken. Neglect was a constant problem. Mrs. Jenkins could be so involved in her own personal problems that she could not spend the enormous amount of time necessary to raise children. Abuse seemed especially likely during withdrawal, as desperation and anger combined to a volatile mixture. Poisoning is a danger in any family, but more so in an addict's family, particularly if there is orange-flavored methadone lying on the kitchen table. Deaths of this kind in an addicted family are not uncommon.

Then why is there a question? Because Mrs. Jenkins could be an excellent mother. She could love her children as much as any other parent, her heroin addiction being no more of a handicap than the evening martini in other families. This is the unknown.

But there was another major question that troubled me: is it right for either Mary or me to decide whether or not Mrs. Jenkins was capable of taking care of her child? Mary and I are sitting back in our offices making this kind of judgment on Mrs. Jenkins from the point of view of how we run our own lives, which may have nothing at all to do with the conditions of hers. Should we have this right? Should anyone?

If there is a suspicion of child abuse, the doctor can easily arrange to have the child removed from the house temporarily by court order. If the case is contested, it goes to court. But this is not a fair system, for poor parents are not accustomed to legal matters and cannot afford the lawyer's fees; rich families almost never lose their children to the court although child abuse is probably just as common as in poor families.

The first patient I had as an intern died as a result of child abuse. She was three years old and had been admitted because of a fractured skull, which we felt was caused by a beating. But it could not be proven in court, and the child went home with the parents. Six months later she was returned to the hospital, dead, having been beaten with a pipe, her head crushed. The other children were removed from the family.

But suppose you are wrong? Suppose a child was not beaten, and you take the child out of the family unjustly? Another patient of mine came onto the accident floor covered with suspicious bruises. I looked up the family in the "Vulnerable Child List," a listing of all families suspected to abuse their children, and saw that the family had been taken to court unsuccessfully for child abuse. Talking to the mother, I had a feeling that this was not child abuse, so I ran a thousand dollars' worth of tests and found out that the child had a very rare bleeding disorder which explained the bruises. For two years the mother had been pursued by the courts unjustly. And the crime would have been worse if the child had been taken out of the family.

But cases with a good resolution are very rare. Usually, you just have a feeling and go by that. Whatever direction you choose to take, someone stands to be hurt, either the child or the family. But perhaps in knowing that, you work harder, following the family closer.

We had decided to let Susan stay in the family if Mrs. Jenkins continued to show interest. Susan and her mother would be helped in every way possible, by Mary and myself, by Susan's grandmother, with support from the housing authority, a psychotherapist, and the drug treatment unit. Perhaps Mrs. Jenkins would find a new, more satisfying life for herself; we would find out as the years passed.

But there were many other roads that could have been taken, and there were no signposts. My discomfort at the decision was eased by knowing that Susan would be staying in the nursery for about a month and that the decision could be changed if necessary. As I watched her shivering with the withdrawal fever, I wondered if this was just the beginning of a lifetime of tragedy for her.

(8)

The only therapy that I could add to what Mary was doing for Mrs. Jenkins was to trust her. The responsibility rested with Mrs. Jenkins for making the changes in her life, and I could only hope it was what she wanted to do. Only she could make use of the services offered to her; she could not be forced to change.

Mrs. Jenkins had been coming to the nursery regularly, from about three to six every afternoon, and with the help of the day nurses she began to get to know her daughter, a child she had been so afraid of that she wanted to give her up for adoption. But she had not really been afraid of her daughter; she had been concerned about what would happen to her, guilty about what had already happened before the child was born. At first she responded stiffly, taking the advice of the nurses as a naughty ten-year-old would accept rebuke. But then she began getting involved with her child and stopped being hostile to the nurses.

Mary had been able to make some changes. She found new housing for Mrs. Jenkins, taking her away from the drug-filled oppressive atmosphere that had surrounded her, and the drug treatment program began having its effect. Mrs. Jenkins was in the methadone treatment program so, although she did not withdraw, she no longer had to get drugs and inject herself. But these changes are hard, something that cannot be genuinely accomplished in a week. Yet talking with Mary, I had the feeling that things were going well, and that Mrs. Jenkins was working to make herself happy in a constructive way.

After a week, Susan's withdrawal slowed down, and she began responding more like a normal child. When she sucked on the nipple, it was no longer the ravenous drive to satisfy some strong internal craving, but the leisurely enjoyment of food and handling much like other children. She was a cute baby, a small face with expression, thin, almost shiny skin, and fine curly blond hair. She had learned to curve her mouth into a wry smile which she would often do just before falling asleep. When she had gas in her stomach, she would have a broad smile.

The jitteriness stopped, and we were able to stop the paregoric after five days. There had been no more diarrhea, and after the IV was removed, she had only a small bald spot to show for it. But the hair would grow back quickly, and I hoped that the other effects of the heroin withdrawal would leave no more of a mark. The culture results from the bacteriology laboratory confirmed that there had been no infection. Although it no longer surprised me, I was amazed at how frightened I had been when Susan first became sick, and how the correct diagnosis had not even occurred to me. If Mrs. Jenkins had not signed out AMA, I wouldn't have guessed the diagnosis for hours. Fortunately, no harm had been done, and next time I would think of it sooner. In fact, from now on, I think I will ask the mother of every newborn I see if she is a heroin addict.

When the culture results came back negative, we took up the adhesive tape that surrounded the crib and took away the clothes rack that held the special gowns. Susan's crib was moved over to the other wall, where she lay among several other babies. She was no longer the nursery outcast, but slept in a row between Baby Boy Hernandez, whose jaundice was improved, and Baby Girl Evans. Pam suggested that in three years these children get together and have an observation nursery reunion. Soy protein formula and applesauce would be served at the gala affair, a courtesy to Baby Evans because she is allergic to milk protein. The decorations would be old adhesive tape, and they would dance around the bili lights of Baby Hernandez.

Mrs. Jenkins was pleased when the tape was removed, because she also felt the isolation. The procedure of putting on the gowns and stepping over the tape had been another symbol of her being different from other mothers, and when it was removed, she may have felt a little less of a stranger.

I talked with Mrs. Jenkins whenever I could, but had little to say about the therapy program that Mary and she had devised. We had become friends.

One night when Susan was about a week old, Mrs. Jenkins came in at about two A.M. Pam and I were busy in the intensive care nursery, and as I looked through the glass into the observation nursery, I noticed that she was crying. I wanted to talk with her, but I could not leave the baby I was with. Alice went to Mrs. Jenkins and asked what the trouble was. Some of her friends had come over to her new house with drugs, and her two life-styles came into conflict: one, the new life that Mrs. Jenkins was trying to reach, and the other, the one she had been accustomed to. The tension of the clash sent her to see her daughter, bringing son Billy with her. He was now asleep in the lobby.

Alice and Mrs. Jenkins became fast friends. That night they talked for five hours, Alice sitting in the rocking chair feeding the babies, Mrs. Jenkins holding her sleeping daughter. At dawn Mrs. Jenkins left with a tired but changed look on her face. I asked Alice what had happened.

"It was the night," Alice answered. "She doesn't know how to handle the nights. That's when it gets bad for her. She is just like me, and we talked about nights. I told her that I learned to deal with the nights by working through them. I used to hate nights; now I sort of like them. She will learn how to get around the nights." Alice began cleaning up the mess in the nurses' station, her usual dawn task. She hates to be cleaning up all the time. No one complains about the mess she leaves around every night, as long as she cleans up once before the day shift comes on.

part iii
Phreddie Martin

(1)

The delivery floor is one of the most peculiar floors in the hospital. It is arranged so that the women in labor lie next to one another in a darkened room, separated by curtains, the moans and screams combining to create an image of confused, drugged pain. At busy times six or eight women might scream in chorus with the pain. When the time has come, and the baby's head is about to appear, the mother is wheeled into a delivery room. When all is well, the baby is sent to the nursery, and the mother to the recovery room, then to the lower floors. It is a custom, a ritual, slowly changing with an occasional father being allowed to see the birth of his child. However, this particular hospital is not that enlightened, and Mr. Martin sat in the waiting room while his wife was in labor.

Mrs. Martin was twenty-eight weeks into her pregnancy, almost seven months along, when she began bleeding from her vagina. She and her husband came to the emergency floor, where she was examined and sent to the delivery floor. She began having mild contractions and soon was in early labor, but still bleeding. Pam and I were called by the obstetricians. We introduced ourselves to Mrs. Martin, stating that we were the pediatricians who would be taking care of her baby, if it happened to be born this soon. After talking with her and listening to the baby's heart through her abdomen, I collected a sample of leaking blood by holding a clean test tube next to her vagina, explaining to her that the test would tell whether it was she or the baby who was bleeding.

"I have lost three children already," she said suddenly as I was about to leave. I had not seen this in the chart and I asked what had happened. "I had three miscarriages, the oldest at about five months. We have been trying to have children for six years now." She seemed embarrassed about what she was saying, perhaps telling me a secret about her body's failure.

"We will do all we can to see that you have a healthy child this time," I answered, assuring her I would be back after the blood test had been done. Pam and I walked slowly back to the nursery.

I told Alice that we might be getting a twenty-eight-week preemie and she said, "I forbid it." Alice always forbade babies from being born sick at night, but it never seemed to do any good. She told me to go back upstairs and tell that baby to stop bleeding and not get born. But she loved children, and knew more pediatrics than most neonatologists, and her wry sense of humor kept the interns and residents sane. At least it always kept us awake. If her imaginings became reality and there ever were two sets of sick triplets born at the same time, I would want Alice to be on duty.

I took the tube of blood to the lab, added some chemicals, and the red color of the blood changed, meaning that there were some fetal blood cells in the tube. This was ominous, as the presence of fetal blood meant the baby was bleeding. Even if labor could be stopped, if the baby continued bleeding it would die of blood loss. The bleeding could be stopped if the baby were delivered, but the infant would be twelve weeks early, and children born this prematurely do not have a very good chance of survival. However, unless the bleeding stopped by itself, there would be no choice. Assuming that the bleeding did not stop, then the baby would be delivered tonight and would probably need an immediate blood transfusion to replace the lost blood. Fortunately, the blood loss was slow, a few drops at a time, but it was continuous. The baby's heart rate was normal, meaning that the blood loss so far was not extensive. We could hope that the bleeding would stop, but there was nothing we could do to make it stop while the baby was still inside.

I told Pam the results of the blood test and she moaned as if having a contraction herself. Another night of no sleep. Nature's time clock and that of humans are not always synchronized. We assumed that the placenta had partially pulled off from the side of the womb, and that this was the cause of the bleeding and the premature labor. We doubted that the bleeding would stop by itself.

We went to the delivery floor and discussed the situation with the obstetricians. The bleeding was a little stronger now, and there was no choice but to try to deliver the baby as soon as possible. Because the baby was so small and Mrs. Martin was in strong labor, I guessed it would be an hour or two. Fortunately, there were no signs of fetal distress, so there was no need for an emergency Caesarian section.

Premature children present problems that are unique to all of medicine. Fetal age is determined by weeks, and a full-term normal baby is about forty weeks old. Baby Martin would be only about twenty-eight weeks, more or less, and its body organs might not be developed enough for independent life. The child's lungs would not be developed enough to exchange air well, and his liver would be unable to exchange toxic elements from his blood. The defenses against infection are very poor. Yet children survive at twenty-eight weeks, and an occasional child will not have any problems at all. With intensive medical care, some children with moderately severe problems do well, growing up to be healthy. But the overall outlook is poor for a child born at this age, and only about 40 percent survive.

Pam and I went through some of the routines in our minds, as we had about two hours to prepare for the hours of work ahead. We obtained blood from the blood bank to give to the baby should he be in shock from blood loss. I called John to tell him of the impending disaster, and of course he was angry at me—as if it were my fault that Mrs. Martin chose our hospital to walk into tonight. He told me to call him in two hours when the child was born, and hung up. He was angry because I woke him up, but he would have been angrier if I hadn't. This way he sleeps for two more hours and feels as if he is on top of the situation.

We went upstairs to check the equipment in the emergency box on the delivery floor, making sure that the oxygen tanks were filled and the necessary drugs present. The two warmer tables were in good condition, and the EKG and blood pressure machines were working well. It was midnight when we walked back into the nursery, having finished our preparations. The nursery was quiet, "too quiet," Alice said. She turned up the radio and started to sing to Baby Boy Sanchez whom she was feeding. She wanted everyone fed before the arrival of this "fetus." She always called a prospective premature infant a fetus, but once the infant was born, she would love it as if it were her own. Alice loved children more than anyone I ever knew, and when she talked to a preemie, the child seemed to listen. Occasionally there were children she did not like, and she would say that she was "allergic" to them.

I walked back up to the labor rooms with the memory of what Mrs. Martin had said about her other three pregnancies weighing on my mind. She was in strong labor, but when I came in she sat up, anxious about what I would have to say. She was still bleeding, but the fetal heart rate was normal. I explained as clearly as I could that the baby was losing blood because the placenta was beginning to separate from the side of her womb, and that this was probably the cause of the premature labor. There was no way that we could stop the bleeding while the baby was still inside, and for both her and the baby's sake, the child would have to be delivered.

"Do babies born this early . . . do they live?" she asked nervously.

I did not know how to answer her question, for her baby had the added problem of blood loss to contend with. I wanted to say that her baby would live, that she would finally have a child after her years of trying, but I could not. "It is too early to tell whether your child will live. About half of all babies born this early live. We will do all we can."

She did not react to the contraction she was having, stunned by the depressing news I had given her. For six and a half months she had been hoping for this baby, praying for a well child, and now she saw tragedy, the same tragedy she had known three times before. She began to cry and I held her hand gently, saying that I was sorry. For the first time I began hoping for a strong, healthy child, not just because it meant less work for me, but because of the joy it would give Mrs. Martin.

"The baby will need a blood transfusion soon after it is born to replace the blood that is being lost," I said after the pause.

"Do what is best for my baby, please."

"I will." As we parted she had another contraction, this time the pain reminding her that her labor would not produce joy, but a very small and probably very sick infant. I told the secretary at the desk to allow Mr. Martin to visit with his wife in the labor room. I would talk to him after the birth, as the obstetricians had already explained the situation to him.

Pam and I knew it would not be possible to try to sleep for the next hour, so Alice went down to the cafeteria to buy some coffee after we reminded her that it was her turn because she had lost that bet on Baby Johnson. And she had to buy the coffee, not just scrounge it up from her friends over on the surgical wards. She had said that it would take Baby Johnson, another preemie, ten days to regain birth weight. Pam said thirteen, and I said fifteen. Pam was right and Alice the furthest away, so she had to buy the coffee. I think this was the first time that Alice ever lost the weight pool—she can look a one-day-old right in the eye and say with all seriousness that he will be healthy until he is eighteen months old, when he will get the chicken pox. She says that she knows how to think like a preemie. While Alice was downstairs, Pam and I did some of the nursing chores. Pam had a tough time on the telephone pretending to be Alice when the nursing supervisor called, wanting to know the census.

We enjoyed the coffee and leisurely talked about this new baby, that it was the fifth in two weeks, that it might be healthy like Baby Sanchez was. But there was a strain in our voices as we were dreading the problems that might arise. We always try to relax when it is not busy in the nursery, unless John is there. When John is around, we become like hyperactive children, running around trying to think of things to do.

The call came about two o'clock; Mrs. Martin was being taken into the delivery room. Pam and I changed into clean scrub suits and washed our hands and arms well. Mrs. Martin recognized us through our caps and masks, smiling when we came into the room. Between contractions, I told her that because the baby was small we would take it right away into the other room that was prepared for the infant, and that we would talk with her as soon as possible after the delivery. She strained to push out the baby.

Pam went into the infant room, turning on the warmer table and the other machines. The emergency kit was opened and the assortment of syringes, drugs, and instruments was carefully placed on the table. A clean endotracheal tube was lying on the side of the table in case it was needed. I was in the delivery room holding a sterile blanket, waiting for the baby. With another push a small head appeared, then the shoulders and arms, then the body covered with amniotic fluid and blood. She was so small! I am always surprised at preemies—they are like miniature babies. As the obstetrician sucked out some of the mucus from her mouth, she began to cry and move about, weak and a little pale, but alive and breathing. As I took her to the other room, I stopped at the head of the delivery table and showed Mrs. Martin her daughter.

The baby was breathing without difficulty, and on the warmer table there was no drop in temperature, which would have been dangerous for the child. But she was pale and her heart rate was faster than normal, her blood pressure low. We knew that she needed blood, so we slowly gave her some of the packed red blood cells through a catheter we placed in her umbilical vein. To cross-match the blood accurately required a sample of the baby's blood and one to two hours, so rather than risk heart failure, we gave her blood that had not been accurately cross-matched, hoping it would not cause any severe problems. After the transfusion she looked better, crying, moving about, breathing at about forty times per minute. Carefully we moved the warmer table down the hall toward the elevator.

When an infant is only twenty-eight weeks old from conception, lung tissue is barely formed. The little air sacs called alveoli which exchange oxygen for carbon dioxide are present, but are small and do not remain open as in older babies. A chemical called surfactant is produced about the twenty-eighth week in fetal life, whose function it is to hold these air sacs open so that oxygen can cross over into the bloodstream. If surfactant has not been made by the time of delivery, the alveoli collapse, preventing the exchange of gases. When this happens, a thick membrane coats the air sacs, making the air exchange even more difficult. This is called hyaline membrane disease, a disease of premature infants and the leading cause of death of infants at this age. Occasionally, babies at twenty-eight weeks will have already manufactured enough surfactant and will not develop the disease, and this was our hope for Baby Girl Martin. But the first six hours of life would tell us for sure.

At birth, babies with this disease often look well, but

they soon begin to breathe rapidly, flaring their noses to get more air in, grunting as the breath is pushed out. As the disease progresses, more air sacs collapse, and the infants have more and more trouble, often breathing one hundred and twenty times a minute, until they die of exhaustion and asphyxiation. If they survive for the first two or three days, the membranes gradually disappear, and if there are no other problems, the children do well. One of the greatest miracles of modern medicine is the ability of science to help these babies through the first two or three days so they survive.

By the time Baby Girl Martin was a half hour old, she had had a transfusion and was in the nursery. She was vigorous, although tiny, and her heart rate had returned to normal after the blood was given. Alice carefully picked her up, supporting her head and back with one hand, and placed her on the scale: 800 grams, about one pound eleven ounces. Carefully she was returned to the warmer table, her legs flopping over Alice's wrist. At first as we worked we did not speak, but as the minutes wore on, we saw that there was no emergency and began to look at this tiny baby rather than at the blood pressure or the EKG machines. Alice began wiping the dried blood and fluid from her face, and the baby grimaced as if looking for a nipple. As I counted the respirations, I saw a beautiful, miniature child . . . a Lilliputian with shiny pink skin covered with tiny white hairs. As the baby lay on her back her legs flopped out to either side. She wrinkled her nose and tried crying again.

"Does she have the 'gray disease'?" Alice asked casually while involved in her work.

"I don't know." I lost count of the respirations, but they were about forty or fifty a minute.

"She's a nice baby . . . sort of looks like a fish, Freddie the fish." As Alice spoke, Baby Girl Martin pursed her tiny lips and blinked her eyes, looking remarkably like a fish.

"O.K., Freddie the Fish Martin it is," I said, gently feeling for her liver and kidneys.

Alice finished repeating the blood pressure and said, "But I wouldn't spell that with an *F* . . . *Ph* instead."

"O.K., Phreddie Martin, welcome to our nursery," Pam said as I laughed, and we began to wrap her heel to do a blood gas. Pam, Alice, and I all knew that nothing in medicine could have made more sense than Baby Girl Martin's new name. She was now a real person.

When Phreddie Martin was about one hour old, she started showing the first signs of hyaline membrane disease, her nose flaring, breathing a little more rapidly. Alice said that she had the disease and I had to agree. After the x-ray technician came, we saw from the chest x-ray that soon Baby Girl Martin would be fighting for her life.

While Pam repeated a thorough examination of the baby, I called John, explaining the situation to him. He told me to follow the blood gases, put in an umbilical artery catheter, and call him if we had any trouble. He was still right on top of the situation. Had this been daytime, he would have been personally conducting every motion our hands made.

In hyaline membrane disease there is usually a steady deterioration for the first two days, with the lungs becoming less and less able to exchange gases. Baby Girl Martin was in the earliest stages, and although we could see that she had the disease, she was doing pretty well. Whether she would worsen rapidly and die in the next six hours, or worsen slowly until she began to recover, we could not tell. But we would soon know.

After warming Phreddie's heel with a warm towel, we drew out some blood for a blood gas and sent some blood to biochemistry for routine tests. Tillie the Terrible snarled at me when I woke her up. I told her that it would be a busy night and not to get upset if I got her counters dirty. I actually talked to Tillie . . . she is part of the staff, and her rank is a lot higher than mine. Residents are a dime a dozen, but a blood gas machine . . .

The blood oxygen was a little low, but not yet enough to add extra oxygen. Baby Girl Martin was alive and breathing, now helplessly trying to suck on the nipple that was placed in her mouth. It was time to think and prepare; there were no reflex actions to do now. She weighed only 800 grams and had the disease, but she was the first living child that the Martins had had. How could I tell them that their beautiful premature infant was probably going to die?

(2)

By four o'clock much of the work had been done. Baby Girl Martin was holding her own, although by looking closely we could detect a slow decline. She was breathing fifty times a minute and had not yet tired out, for she moved about on the warmer table actively. We could see that she was having some trouble pulling air into her lungs because she was beginning to use her chest muscles—with every breath you could faintly see the outline of her ribs. But she was pink and still had the energy to cry and suck on the nipple.

Pam had taken cultures of the infant's skin, mouth, umbilical cord, and blood, looking for an infection. Because the risk of infection was high, we started Phreddie on two antibiotics, for she was too weak to resist an infection if one were present. Pam was able to put in the umbilical artery catheter easily, and the x-ray showed it to be in good position. We now had in a "line" through which we could draw out arterial blood for the blood gas measurements which we might be doing as often as every fifteen minutes later on. When we weren't using the catheter to draw out blood, it was used to give intravenous fluids, transfusions, and medications, particularly bicarbonate.

The last blood gas we had done showed a blood oxygen of forty, which was beginning to get low. Therefore, a clear plastic dome or "hood" with a hole cut in it for the neck was placed over her head and extra oxygen was added to the air she was breathing. Because Phreddie was so small we had to pad the areas around the neck hole with towels to prevent the added oxygen from escaping.

It is hard to describe what it is like to take care of a one-pound-eleven-ounce premature baby. As an intern, I was terrified of preemies because they looked so fragile, and I might still be terrified today if Alice hadn't reminded me that preemies were afraid of the doctors because they were so big. Peemies are people, small people, but humans just the same. During the hour that slowly passed I began to get acquainted with Phreddie, seeing how she was different from other preemies, how she had a certain way of curling her toes that I had never seen before. But her toes were small, frighteningly small, and she had an illness that would probably prove to be fatal. This was what was most frightening—the fact that she would die and her parents remain childless. Alice had ominous feelings about this baby, feelings she could not describe, but she was wishing that we hadn't named her.

Alice named most of the babies in the nursery, particularly the long timers. She had an aversion to the titles "Baby Boy" and "Baby Girl" because they had nothing to do with the individual child. Baby Boy Jackson soon became Wild Man Jackson because of the angry way he had of demanding his formula. But when Mrs. Jackson told us her son's name was Thomas, we all called him Tom, because that was his name, Tom Wild Man Jackson. We didn't want any of our patients growing up without knowing their real names, but until the mother supplied one, we made one up ourselves.

But you don't want to make up a name for a child you want to stay away from. That's why we were reluctant about "Phreddie." We knew that the odds against her were now up to about ten to one, and we didn't want to get too close. She was still a fetus, too small to be human, and if she died, she would just be an anonymous abortion.

Pam and I were beginning to tire, momentarily, as

we now had a chance to sit. Alice, assuming that part of her job was to keep us awake and happy, put a baby in Pam's lap, handed her a bottle, opened the window, turned up the radio, and went out on the obstetrical floors to scrounge up some coffee. Alice had been the intern and resident "psychiatrist" for ten years, enjoying this job and doing it well, for instead of getting sleepier, we began thinking of the work yet to be done. Alice returned with a tray of coffee and one half-eaten brownie, which we split three ways.

Standing by the heating table in the center of the room, I watched Phreddie Martin breathe. Through the hood I saw her opening her eyes, now looking anxious because it was hard to breathe. At the end of each breath she gave a barely audible grunt, then, using all her strength, she pulled air in. Her arms and legs lay still, outstretched on the table—she was beginning to tire.

Using a small syringe, I drew out some arterial blood from the catheter, and while Pam checked the blood for an anemia, I did a blood gas. The oxygen was up to 55 percent in the blood with the hood, just where we wanted it. However, the value for carbon dioxide was getting higher, another sign that she was getting worse. But we knew that she was getting worse and would continue to worsen for the next two days—why was I surprised? I guess, because I was hoping so hard that she would start to get better, I was disappointed by the reality.

I had not yet returned to talk with Mrs. Martin about her daughter, something that, although I must do it, I wanted to avoid. We had been busy, but now there was time, and the ominous news that I would have to give about hyaline membrane disease would be hard for her. I slowly walked toward the door, about to go upstairs, when the phone rang. Alice answered and called out, "Preemie twins, delivering now . . ."

I was stunned. Then, running to the table for my stethoscope, I yelled out, "Call Dennis on the accident floor . . . and call John. Put the oxygen at forty for her,

and . . . get some more bicarb and syringes upstairs."
Pam had already run out the door toward the stairway.
As I ran past Tillie's room I said a silent prayer, "Please
don't break tonight."

(3)

The call from the delivery floor was our daily fear. We could hope that the twins would be big, perhaps thirty-six weeks or so—they hadn't told us on the phone—but if they were tiny or sick, there was no way that Pam and I alone could give good care because we were not prepared. Dennis, another resident, would come over from the emergency floor, and John would come in, but that would take about fifteen minutes. Both heating tables were on the delivery floor, as the one Baby Martin had used had been returned. We had not replaced the equipment we had used in the emergency kit; hopefully there would be enough there. Pam arrived first and went straight to the infant room, beginning to set up—it was all reflex, the kind of disaster we worry about every minute on duty. I would not think about Phreddie Martin until things were stable here; Alice would take care of her while we were gone. I went straight to the delivery room.

Frank, the obstetrical resident, was gowned and gloved at the foot of the delivery table, and when I came in he said, "Just came in, about thirty weeks along, twins, and the fetal hearts irregular and slow." There had not been enough time to give the mother a spinal, and with a scream she pushed and the first baby was born. The cord was quickly cut and the child placed into the sterile towel I was holding.

The child was tiny, smaller than the assumed thirty weeks, smaller even than Baby Martin had been, and as I went into the other room, the child did not start to breathe. As I lay the flaccid, tiny infant on the table, Pam began sucking the mucus out of his mouth, then held the oxygen over his head. I listened for the heart rate and it was very low at about twenty; there was no pulse. A few slaps on the feet did nothing, and the child started to turn blue.

"Give cardiac massage while I intubate," I said as I turned to the other table to get the smallest-size endotracheal tube. Pam pressed her fingers over the infant's heart rapidly, about eighty times a minute, to create a heartbeat, as I held the child's mouth open with the laryngoscope and passed the tube between the tiny vocal cords. Putting my lips around the tube, I pushed three short breaths into the baby's lungs gently, as I did not want to put too much pressure on the fragile lungs. I was about to get some bicarbonate when the second child, also not breathing, was brought in by the obstetrician. He was only slightly bigger than the first and was placed on the other heating table. "Stay here," I said to Pam, handing her the tube and the wall oxygen line. She continued beating the heart and breathing for the infant while I went to the other table.

Because there were two children, I would take care of the larger as I had had more experience and the larger had a better chance of survival. When I left the other table, I knew the smaller baby would soon be dead, for Pam did not have enough hands to do all that was necessary.

The larger child was not breathing and looked to be about twenty-six weeks along. If we could just start them breathing, and bring back the heart rate, we could worry about all the other problems later. Frank said that the heart rate was about fifty, and I started to get the other endotracheal tube. Dennis ran in, stopping briefly at the table with the smaller baby, then coming over to the baby I was working on, the gray color of the first baby telling him that it was hopeless. He began giving cardiac massage to try to circulate the blood while the heart was not beating strongly. Again I opened the baby's mouth to pass the tube, but there was a pool of mucus and I could not see the vocal cords. After sucking out some of the mucus I passed the tube, but after giving some oxygen, the baby continued to get gray. Dennis listened with his stethoscope over the baby's stomach and, because of the sounds, knew that the tube was not in the lungs but in the esophagus. I pulled the tube and this time passed it through the vocal cords into the windpipe. But the heart rate was very low, the baby's color ashen. The baby on the other table was a deep purple color.

"Pam," I said, "leave it . . . we need six cc.'s of bicarb here." She realized that her efforts were in vain, but it was hard to leave the child who was still alive and turn to the other. But if she didn't help here, both children would certainly die. I made the choice; we would put all our efforts into this larger baby. There were now three of us working on the child, and the obstetrician walked out of the room after covering the smaller twin with a towel.

About ten minutes later John ran in. The preemie was still gray and had a low heart beat, but was alive. He probably weighed one and a half pounds. We tried everything we knew to bring him back, injecting epinephrine and calcium directly into his heart, cardiac massage, bicarbonate, but it was not working. He was barely alive now, but would not be for long unless we could get some oxygen into his blood. John began giving the orders and we tried everything a second time, frantically, four doctors and two nurses trying to save the life of this child. But his heart no longer beat by itself at all, and after another fifteen minutes of desperation measures, we began to slow down, realizing that the child was dead, that there was nothing more we could do. I walked out into the hallway, and the obstetrician told the babies' mother that both children had died.

"What happened?" John asked finally.

"I don't know," I replied, exhausted. "She just came in off the street and the heart rates were slow and irregular, and when she delivered, the infants did not breathe." The irregular heartbeats told us that even before birth the children were not getting enough oxygen. They were almost dead by the time they were born, and there was nothing that we could do to save them. Two children died.

I did not want to talk. I wanted to go into another room and go to sleep or disappear. I wanted to yell with anger and cry softly, but I could only walk down the hall.

"They were too young," John said as I walked away.

(4)

Death is part of my job; doctors see people die all the time. When a patient dies, I have to come to terms with it. I see and feel the parents' sadness, and for a period of time I live with the sadness. Yet, because of my job, I could not let the feelings I had interfere with what I had to do now. The twins' parents would mourn for a long time, but I was not able to do so. I had to complete my mourning by the time I finished my cigarette in the room beside the nursery, for when I came out I would have to put all my strength into taking care of Phreddie Martin. There was no room for the self doubt I was feeling—if the tube had been placed properly the first time, would that second twin be alive? If Dr. Williams had been there, would the children be alive? The questions were distracting. I had to forget them, put them, unresolved, out of my mind. Doctors are not supposed to be sentimental. As I put out my cigarette, I became thankful that Phreddie Martin was as big as she was.

John and Pam were talking about Baby Girl Martin. As I drew out some blood for a blood gas, I could see that she was struggling more, but had not worsened drastically in the time we were gone. The changes were slow—I guess we could be thankful for that. Phreddie looked exhausted; every breath was very hard work, and she would not be

(129)

able to keep it up much longer. When she breathed, you could clearly see all her ribs, and her neck muscles strained. The blood gas was ominous: the oxygen was low, and the carbon dioxide very high because the gas exchange in her lungs was so poor. It would not be long before she needed the respirator, and a preemie who has to go on the respirator by six hours of age does not have much chance of survival.

Pam and John increased the amount of oxygen that was going into the plastic hood over Baby Martin's head, and I walked upstairs to talk with Mrs. Martin. The first light of dawn was beginning to show outside.

My mind was working slowly as I took the elevator upstairs; it felt like glue. Mrs. Martin was asleep when I walked in but woke up as soon as I touched her on the arm.

"Is she alive?" she asked.

"Yes, your daughter is alive, but she is not doing very well." I went on to explain hyaline membrane disease, as clearly as I could, and that the baby would soon need a machine, the respirator, to breathe. I was too tired to explain things properly, and I could not anticipate her questions and answer them, even though she would not ask them. We sat silently for a few moments.

"I will come back soon and we can talk more. We will do everything possible," I reassured her.

As I walked back down the hallway toward the elevator I thought of stopping in to see Mrs. Bates, the mother of the twins. A man approached me and asked if I was the pediatrician. I said yes.

"How is my baby?" he asked.

I became confused. A million conflicting thoughts raced through my mind, unsorted. I had never seen this man before—was he Mr. Martin or Mr. Bates? I tried to remember if he said "baby" or "babies." I was numb, and in the two seconds that passed all I could think was static. I began to feel a cold sweat. "Excuse me, your name is . . . ?"

"Mr. Martin. My wife had a baby girl this evening."

I became even more confused, beginning to panic. Was it Baby Girl Bates and Twin Martin or the other way around? Who was alive? Another second passed, my face expressionless. But reason began to create order in my confused brain. He had a baby this evening and it was the twins who died, so he must be the father of the child who is living, Phreddie's father. Now I knew who he was and wanted to jump up and down, saying that his daughter was alive, that she was breathing and had a heartbeat and everything. But Phreddie was sick, and in another expressionless second I realized what I would have to say.

"Perhaps we could go over here and sit down," I said, and during the short walk, order returned to my thinking. We sat by the window, and I explained to him what I had said to Mrs. Martin. His daughter was a very small premature baby and had hyaline membrane disease. We talked for about fifteen minutes, and the bright sun of morning broke through the window. I thought to myself that I had almost gone completely crazy, berserk because I couldn't remember who was living and who had died.

In the nursery the dawn's sunlight was streaming through the windows and Alice was busy cleaning up the counters. She was mumbling to herself the way she often does when John is around, as he is not one of her favorites. She is allergic to him. Pam and John were getting the respirator ready, and while they were doing that, I examined Phreddie again.

She was so small, only a handful. When I examined her legs, my hands were only a couple of inches away from the top of her head. And she was alive. I thought of the twins briefly as I looked at Phreddie. I wanted this child to live more than I ever wanted anything in the world. In a sense I wanted to avenge the death of the twins by enabling Phreddie to grow up to become a normal person.

Baby Girl Martin was readied to go on the respirator, because she could no longer breathe for herself adequately. We would intubate her (put a tube down into her airway) and, with the machine, deliver oxygen at such a pressure as to keep her air sacs open. The pressure would force air across the hyaline membranes that were forming, and hopefully enough oxygen would get into her blood to keep her alive until she began healing by herself. It sounds rather simple, but the respirator is dangerous, and her outlook was still poor. Because the pressure was high, there was a constant risk of blowing out one of the infant's lungs, and with a collapsed lung, no air could get in. Also, there were problems with infection and chemical changes in the blood. Nonetheless, the respirator was the baby's only hope, so the risks were inconsequential.

Pam would pass the tube, with John's help, and I would hold Phreddie. We placed a pillow under her neck, a towel folded over once, so Pam could get a clear view of the vocal cords. Alice held the suctioning equipment to remove the mucus. I held the child's arms tight against her chest, watching the EKG machine and making sure that all was well. This was not an emergency; we could do it slowly and carefully, because Phreddie could live on her own for a while longer. Using a very small tube, Pam placed it in the trachea, with John giving constant advice, and the respirator was attached. The tube was taped into Phreddie's mouth, and at first she began to suck on it a little. But it was uncomfortable for her, and when she cried, no sounds came out. The machine hummed and pushed in a breath every few seconds, but the baby did not understand that she could now relax and let the machine do the work. Instead she fought the tube, trying to breathe by herself. This is dangerous for the baby because it puts an enormous amount of pressure on the fragile lungs, and if she should be trying to breathe out when the machine pushes air in, her lungs could burst. To prevent this, we gave her a large shot of morphine which made her stop breathing. We purposely overdosed her with narcotics to let the machine do the work.

An x-ray was taken which showed the tube to be in the proper place, and it also showed the worsening of the hyaline membrane disease. Her lungs looked white on the film, as white as the bones. You could not tell where the heart was anymore because the lungs were so white.

After taking a few blood gas measurements we had adjusted the dials of the machine to deliver the proper amount of oxygen at the right pressure. The pressure setting was critical, and it was set at the lowest possible figure to keep the blood oxygen high. We were now at a pressure of six, with 40 percent oxygen in the air that was passing down the tube. Normal air is 20 percent oxygen. The baby lay on the table, eyes closed, motionless except for her chest, which rose every time the machine made its clicking sound.

After doing another blood test for blood volume, we transfused a small amount of blood into Phreddie to replace the blood we were using for our tests. We sent some blood down to the biochemistry lab to check for jaundice and calcium. It was getting close to coffee time and we were slowing down again. John was talking about the movie he had been to the previous night, before the twins were born, and about the new kind of respirators they were using in another hospital. I heard him speak clearly, but the words made absolutely no impression on my mind; it was like listening to the sounds of the respirator. Alice stayed in the other room as much as possible. "I don't want to have to get nasty with that boy," she would say. John never knew why Alice didn't like him.

(5)

By seven in the morning, Baby Girl Martin was again "stable," the machine efficiently breathing for her diseased lungs. She was now five hours old, and as I watched her lying on the warmer table, I wondered why we were working so hard on this baby who was going to die. But John was convinced we were going to save her, despite all the odds. It was a personal challenge for him and he would devote all his knowledge and energy to help us save Phreddie Martin. He had not met the parents, nor had he any desire to. His interest was in statistics; it was a matter of prestige to be able to "pull off" an 800-gram twenty-eight-week preemie with hyaline membrane disease. It would look great on his curriculum vitae. When I was tired, I became cynical about John's motivation. I had no idea at all of my own motivation.

By the time Emily and Steve came in, Phreddie Martin was receiving 40 percent oxygen at a pressure of seven. As the disease worsened in her lungs, both the pressure and the percentage of oxygen would rise to try to keep her supplied with oxygen. Because the infant was knocked out with morphine, she did not struggle against the machine that was breathing for her. So far, there did not seem to be any major complications: there had been no bleeding within the brain, as we had done a spinal tap and found no blood. The endotracheal tube was in the proper place and had not slipped. There were no signs of infection, but we were treating her for infection just in case. The umbilical artery catheter was in the proper place, as checked by x-ray, and had not clotted off as sometimes will happen. The anemia had been initially corrected on the delivery floor, and the small transfusions we were giving her replaced the blood we were taking for tests. Multiple tests for sugar, calcium, and other substances were within normal limits. Aside from the probably fatal disease in her lungs, she was doing quite well. But her lungs continued to deteriorate.

As usual, the coffee and doughnuts arrived just when we needed them most. My joy at seeing Em and Steve arrive was due mainly to the knowledge that I couldn't make decisions anymore. I had wondered why we were working so hard on Phreddie Martin. I had lost my reason, and I really could not answer that question. If I had not been exhausted, I would not have asked it. There had been two kinds of work during the night. One was the physical exhaustion of running from floor to floor, taking blood samples to the biochemistry lab and blood bank. In one sense it is good that there is a lot of legwork, for it relaxes you from the second kind of work, the emotional exhaustion of continuous thinking, seeing patients die, talking with parents, and making the never-ending decisions.

The ritual of the coffee and doughnuts, the only ritual in the world worth preserving, brings new hope into your life, the hope of being able, at some time in the future, to go home to sleep. Steve and Emily did not look through the glass in the nursery until they had settled themselves and begun drinking the coffee. Emily got up and went over to get some more sugar.

"Oh, no . . . had a bad night, huh?" Steve said as he peered through the glass.

He could see the tiny infant on the respirator; of course that means a bad night. "Eight hundred grams," I said, "and we lost a pair of twins." He could tell by the tone of my voice that he would have to be careful what he said to me. He would have enough work taking care of that fetus over there; he didn't need a crazy resident to take care of also.

I was depressed, telling them about the twins without emotion. I wanted to get away from the nursery, quit medicine, break all ties with anything that related to the evening before. I did not want to see Phreddie Martin again because she was going to die. I didn't have to take care of her now. I had been close to her during the night, watching her, hoping that she would live, but now that emotion turned to hate. I did not care if she lived; I made believe, in my own mind, that she was already dead. I wanted to go home and sleep for a week.

We cut short our time over coffee because of the amount of work to be done. As usual, we started with the babies who were not critically ill, and the scut book began to fill with the routine jobs that had to be done. Pam and I did not speak often; we trailed around, trying to absorb some of Emily and Steve's enthusiasm, but it was hopeless.

After rounds, Emily stayed with Phreddie Martin. She repeated the blood gases frequently, made the changes in the respirator settings as the infant worsened throughout the day. I spent my time doing routine chores, slowly, without looking at the preemie.

When Mr. and Mrs. Martin came into the nursery late in the morning, I explained to them how the baby was doing. They looked sadly at their motionless infant, and the huge machine that was breathing for her, and left the nursery. They had not chosen a name for her yet, as they first wanted to know if she would live. I had introduced Emily to them, and she would also assume the duty of talking to the parents for the rest of the day and night.

The day passed very rapidly for me as I was in an emotionless haze. The chores were done, one at a time, until they were finished. When Emily told me that she raised the oxygen to 60 percent, I did not say anything, and at five in the afternoon I left the nursery without looking in the corner where Phreddie Martin's heating table was, knowing that when I returned in the morning I would not hear the monotonous drone of the respirator.

(6)

As usual, the night off went by quickly, and I arrived the next morning with Pam, who had brought the coffee. It was a new day, I was rested, and I assumed that the premature baby I was working on the day before was dead by now. I looked into the special care nursery, and Baby Girl Martin was in exactly the same position she had been in the evening before, the respirator still going.

"How's she doing?" I asked casually, drinking the coffee, a little confused because Phreddie was not dead.

"She's hanging in there," Emily answered. "The oxygen is up to eighty percent and the pressure is at nine, and she's good. A little jaundiced, though."

"How was your night?" asked Pam. I sat quietly, trying to reason why Phreddie was doing so well.

"Not too bad. We were up every hour or so to do gases, but we got some sleep." We had all mastered the art of falling asleep instantly, so that if there was a free hour without having to do tests, we would get one hour of sleep, exactly.

There were some routine problems found during work rounds, but the day looked quiet. Perhaps Emily and Steve would be able to get home in the early afternoon. The four of us talked at length at Phreddie's bedside about the changes that had occurred during the night and why she was doing comparatively well. Steve said that Alice had begun spending more time with Phreddie, which we recognized as a very good prognostic sign. Alice often avoids those babies who are going to die. Of course, Steve and Emily had approved of the name Phreddie, because Alice's names are always fitting. Her own three children are named Paul, Marsha, and David. What a relief!

As we stood by the table, I was filled with a new hope that erased the confusion and the conflicts. The child was not only alive, but had not worsened nearly as much as we were expecting. The oxygen level was only eighty and the pressure was at nine, still well within the safe range. I had anticipated that the oxygen would be at least to 100 percent and the pressure very high, if she were alive at all. This was very good news, because it meant that not only could we still treat her if she got worse, but perhaps the disease in her lungs was beginning to rebate. Perhaps she would live.

I saw her small hands lying outstretched on the table and thought of her parents who had wanted a child for six years. I saw her red, abraded skin where tape had been, and her puffy, small eyes, knowing that I had been foolish to believe, maybe even hope, that this child would die. Even though her chance of surviving was still very slim, there was a chance, there had always been a chance, and I would concentrate on that chance rather than the odds.

The yesterday feelings had faded—I no longer wanted to avoid this infant. My mind was rested, and I searched for things we could and should do for her. Phreddie was a beautiful tiny infant who would be dead now if it hadn't been for us. I had done my job correctly the night she was born, and she could still grow up to be a beautiful lady. She had a cute nose even if the rest of her was a little scrawny. By the time she was five months old she wouldn't look like a fish and no one would think to call her "Phreddie." She became my patient again, and for the first time I was wide awake and enthusiastic, ready to work hard to do all that was possible to save her life. We could save her; John's dream would come true.

I worked eagerly, efficiently. The decisions were easy, and John's advice was good. I didn't mind the way he ordered me to take his advice, a tolerance I don't feel when I am tired. Phreddie was stable and doing fairly well when the delivery floor called and asked us to come up. Emily would watch Phreddie while we were gone.

We took the elevator, conserving our strength for the long day, as there was no "stat" in the delivery floor call. A mother was delivering, and the amniotic fluid that came out when her membranes ruptured smelled of an infection. We took some of the fluid and examined it with stains, and there were bacteria present. When the baby delivered, he cried and seemed all right, so I left Pam with him and went back to the nursery. Pam spent the rest of the morning taking cultures from the new baby to see if he was infected, and began antibiotics. It turned out that the baby had a pneumonia, but did well.

During the day, Mrs. Martin came into the nursery often to see her daughter. She quickly recognized the hope in my voice and began to believe that the child would live in spite of my saying that it was far too early to tell. I talked with her frequently during the day, and she kept repeating, "She's so small," as she looked about the nursery at all the regular-sized babies. But she was getting to know her daughter, her fear lessening, and as we talked, she began to understand hyaline membrane disease and the respirator therapy we were giving the child. There had been a repeat chest x-ray, and I was able to say that it had gotten no worse.

Phreddie did quite well, considering. She was now thirty-five hours old, the oxygen was up to 90 percent, and the pressure at eleven. Because the carbon dioxide was still rising in her blood, we increased the volume of air going into her lungs, and this worked well. But we were beginning to get into dangerous territory, because a pressure of eleven is very high, almost high enough to blow out a lung. If a lung were to collapse, it was doubtful that we could re-expand it in time to save her. This is the most dreaded complication of respirator therapy, called a pneumothorax. A pressure of eleven shouldn't cause a pneumothorax, but it was getting very close.

Phreddie was beginning to look quite jaundiced, and the blood test we had sent to the lab returned and was nine. This was a real worry, for jaundice, or bilirubin, if it is high, can cause brain damage, called kernicterus. The bilirubin in a high enough concentration attaches to brain cells and destroys them. In preemies, a bilirubin level of fifteen is considered the beginning of brain damage. In full-term babies the value can go higher before damage begins.

There were several possible reasons for the jaundice. The most likely was because the baby's liver had not yet fully developed, and bilirubin, which comes from blood cells, could not be removed as it normally is. Babies born at nine months can also have jaundice for this reason, but not as severely. A second possibility for the jaundice was that we gave Baby Martin a blood transfusion on the delivery floor without accurately cross-matching the blood. If there had been a transfusion reaction, some of the blood cells would break down, thus causing an increase in the level of bilirubin. I felt that both factors were involved here. We sent off a number of blood tests to rule out other possibilities.

Without waiting for any further tests, we began therapy for the jaundice by placing Phreddie "under the lights." The lights are a rack of fluorescent light bulbs which are placed next to the baby, as it is known that bright light breaks down the bilirubin. But we were afraid that this would not be enough and prepared for an exchange transfusion, replacing all of the infant's blood with fresh blood that has no bilirubin in it. This, of course, is done slowly over a period of time and can be dangerous for preemies, as there are a multitude of secondary problems that can occur. But again, there would be no choice. If the bilirubin got too high, the brain damage could kill

Phreddie as fast as any of the complications of the exchange transfusion.

Three hours later the bilirubin level had jumped to sixteen, so we began the exchange. Ten cc.'s of Phreddie's blood out, ten cc.'s of new blood in, repeated over and over, slowly, carefully, checking the calcium levels often, being careful not to let any air get into the blood. In a few hours it was completed, and there did not seem to be any of the dreaded problems. The child continued to lie on the table, being breathed for by the respirator, now a morphine addict because the drug was being given so often.

After the exchange transfusion, Phreddie went back under the lights, or back to "the Riviera," as Alice called it. Phreddie Martin was sunning herself on the Riviera, euphoric from the morphine, being breathed for, having every care attended. Of course, she wore protective eyeshades, as all true sunbathers do.

As the day wore on, the changes were slow. The jaundice levels remained normal, but her oxygen again began to get low. We raised the oxygen up to 100 percent, pure oxygen; we were now at the limit. Raising the pressure further would be very dangerous, and we could not raise the oxygen. She would have to start improving soon, for we had no therapy beyond this. And it was time for her to start improving. But the blood gases during the day did not change.

(7)

It was about six in the evening, and Steve and Emily had gone home. It was quiet; Phreddie Martin was the only critical patient in the nursery. Otherwise, except for the baby with the pneumonia, everybody was pretty healthy, other preemies growing and gaining weight, slowly approaching the magic five-pound mark when they could go home. We didn't want any fat, healthy preemies hanging around our nursery.

Pam and I had been working hard with Baby Girl Martin all afternoon. We spent all our time with her, doing the exchange transfusion, watching the respirator, doing blood tests. She was nearing the height of her disease; the textbooks said she should start getting better any time now. It would be slow, perhaps taking several weeks, but her lungs should start to improve. Unfortunately, she was near the limit of what we could do to help her, and if she got much worse, she would die. Phreddie was a real person to us, incredibly tiny and very sick, but a real person just the same. We had grown to know and love this baby, lying there dwarfed by the giant respirator. She would move slightly on occasion, and we looked into her face a thousand times. Pam put a fresh bandage over her umbilical stump.

The nursery door opened and an incubator was wheeled in. We saw inside of it a little white towel covering something. A miniature foot was showing from under the towel, a foot half the size of Phreddie's. We knew what had happened, so we turned away and began working with Phreddie again. The obstetrical nurse told the nursery staff that the baby was about twenty weeks along, a miscarriage. There had been no way they could have prevented the birth. But the child was still a newborn, and the heart was beating, so he was transferred to pediatrics. We had not been called for the delivery because there was no chance to save a baby this small, and he would live here in the nursery until he died—or at least until his heart stopped beating. We did not want to see the fetus—no one did—so he was covered with a towel; I wished that the foot had been covered also.

Linda, the nurse on duty, took the baby out of the incubator and placed him on a table in the corner. She listened to the heartbeat and weighed him on a scale, recording both on the paper beside the table. He would be our patient for the half hour or so that he lived. The infant weighed 380 grams, less than a pound, and Linda carried him in one hand, his arms and legs falling through her fingers, miniature gray arms and legs.

I looked again at Phreddie, a giant compared to this new admission, but not all that different. I went to the other table and examined the dying fetus because I had to. He was an admission and, like all the others, had to be worked up, all the paper work done. Phreddie was stable at the moment and Pam took care of her.

The dying baby was still warm and his heart was beating, about twenty beats per minute, regular, slow beats. He was not breathing and was gray-blue. Microscopic fingers that made a pencil look like a telephone pole did not move. The eyes were still fused shut, a little crease in the skin where eyelids would have soon formed; he would never see daylight because his eyes had not yet formed. But he was a person, a person so small that life was not possible with today's medical care—he had no right to be born this early. The obstetrician, in order to spare the mother anguish, had probably already told her that her son was dead.

I do not remember this baby's name. This was not a baby I was going to get excited about; it would have been a waste of emotional energy. This was just one of nature's little tragedies and there was nothing we could do about it now. Babies this young are not frequent admissions to the nursery, but are certainly not rare. I put the baby in an incubator and kept the temperature high so his body temperature would be 98°. I knew this was going to make the baby die sooner than if he got cold, for with a normal body temperature energy is used up more rapidly and the heart stops sooner than if the body temperature were down at 80°. Was this euthanasia, murder? No. Just routine medical care; newborn babies are put into incubators. But without this routine care, his life would be fifteen minutes longer, increasing his life-span by 50 percent. Of course he would die either way, but what I did probably made him die sooner.

At the time I certainly did not consider this euthanasia. He was not suffering, for there was no consciousness that could recognize agony. I did not really consider this child alive, even though he had a heartbeat. Is life determined by the present, that is, the presence of a heartbeat, or the future, the knowledge that the heartbeat would stop in a few minutes regardless of what the most talented physician did? I do not know the meaning of the word or concept "life," even though my job is partly to preserve it. But with this child, rather than to preserve or prolong what seemed to me to be meaningless "life," I put him in the incubator and caused him to die sooner. I am now very ashamed of this because what I did was not to spare this infant suffering—he was too young to feel it—but to spare myself the anguish of waiting for him to die.

The baby had been baptized on the delivery floor by the obstetrical nurses as soon as he was aborted because the parents were Catholic. A priest came into the nursery, and the child was baptized again. The priest came often to the nursery, always to see the dying; he never spent time with the healthy babies. But he could do far more for our new patient and his family than we could, and although I do not understand his religion, I was happy to see him.

The child would be called an abortion, a miscarriage, a preemie, or a child who died, according to your point of view. We spend little time in pediatrics discussing the terminology, because we ignore the issue of abortion. Usually, when we are asked to help, the decision of whether or not a child should live has already been made. Questions such as whether abortions are good or bad, and the definition of life, we try to avoid—just like the rest of the medical profession.

But what exactly is the difference between a three-inch abortus and Phreddie Martin, whom I was coming to love? Only about ten inches and one and a half pounds. We were working so hard to save Phreddie, who in a sense was a spontaneous abortion, yet cared little for the medically performed abortions. I have difficulty coming to understand even the very simple moral questions; I am overwhelmed by these complex issues.

The priest stopped momentarily before Phreddie Martin's table, seeming to say a silent prayer. He took off his nursery robes and looked again like a priest. He would go and talk with the infant's mother about her dead son. He could do more for her than a thousand doctors.

After a while I checked the baby's heart rate again, and there was none. I pronounced the infant dead and filled out the papers, listing the cause of death as "Prematurity—20 weeks." I carried the papers down to the front desk of the hospital, my long white nursery gown flowing through the silent midnight corridors like some angel of death.

The clerk took the papers and as he filed them casually asked, "Another preemie, huh?"

(8)

By one in the morning the nursery was again quiet, and our time was spent with the routine work that seemed endless. Baby Girl Martin was stable, so we went around to all the babies, checking for problems. We called the lab for the results of the latest bilirubin tests on Phreddie and another baby. The previous bili was down to five after the exchange transfusion, which we expected, and we hoped that it would not climb too high. There was more blood in the blood bank, just in case we had to repeat the exchange, but we hoped that her being on "the Riviera" would prevent that. The other test showed that the cause of jaundice was the blood we had given her on the delivery floor. But had we not given her that blood, she might have died, so instead we caused a problem that we would have to treat later.

I walked into Tillie's room with a handful of small tubes to do a routine blood gas. We were repeating them every hour, and they were slowly getting worse. This one showed that the blood oxygen was again getting dangerously low, even though she was now breathing pure oxygen. There was no way that we could increase the oxygen as we had done before—she was at the maximum. The expression on my face as I returned to the nursery told Pam that we would have to make a difficult decision. The respirator pressure was now set at eleven, which was dangerously high anyway. The only way that we could think of raising the amount of oxygen in the baby's blood was to increase the pressure even further. We would push the oxygen into her blood any way we could, but this, we both knew, would probably be fatal. The lungs could stand only so much pressure, and we were exceeding that. The result would be that we would rupture the lungs and the baby would die. But she would die if we did not raise the pressure, and babies have been known to live with respirator pressures up to 13. Very few, very lucky babies.

I called John and told him of the results of the blood gas. He wasn't any more enthusiastic about it than I was but said, "O.K., pump her up." I raised the pressure to 13, maintaining the same volume of air going into her lungs. She was still receiving 100 percent oxygen. As I turned up the dial, I felt that her lungs would explode like an overfilled balloon before me, and she would then quickly turn gray. If this were to happen, we had the equipment ready to put in chest tubes to try to re-expand her lungs, but we knew that would not work and the baby would quickly die. Five, ten minutes went by, and there was no change; she just lay there, her color pink. We repeated the blood gas test.

This showed a good rise in the blood oxygen, well within the safe range, and fifteen minutes had gone by without a pneumothorax. She was a strong infant, a fragile, strong, tiny newborn. She was also becoming a morphine addict as we gave her more to keep her from waking up and trying to breathe for herself. If she did that, the pressure in her lungs would surely increase and her lungs would collapse. Now we could only sit and wait to see what would happen. Only wait: if she continued to get worse without getting a pneumothorax, there was nothing further we could do.

Phreddie Martin was alive. She was a real living person to me. I had come to know her well in a special way. If it hadn't been for medical science she would be dead, and although she could die at any minute, there was still the faint hope that she could grow up to be a normal adult. While many very small preemies are retarded, there had been nothing to suggest that Phreddie would be: the jaundice had not become too high; the oxygen, so far, had not been too low; there had been no bleeding in the brain.

The possibility that she would grow up as a retarded child was difficult to ignore, however. But I concentrated on my hopes that she would instead become a ballet dancer, or an artist, or a college professor, or a mature woman who would live her life fully, with all its joys and sorrows, recognizing life as the miracle it is.

Pam stayed with Phreddie and I walked up to the maternity floor. Mrs. Martin was lying in bed, the lights off; I thought she was sleeping.

"You've come to tell me that she died," she said through the dark.

"No, your daughter is still living." I walked in and sat by the chair next to the bed. She did not turn the light on, and my eyes adjusted to the dark. I held her hand as she cried wordlessly. She had wanted to cry so many times and was prepared to cry now, but the tears flowed anyway, even though her daughter was still alive.

"She's so small . . . I was afraid of her today when I saw her. She doesn't look alive . . . she doesn't move, and all those tubes in her. If she lives, will I always be afraid to touch her?"

"Only if you allow yourself to hold on to that fear." I wanted to explain further, but I couldn't. It was better just to sit there and hold hands.

"I will be going home tomorrow." She was trying to dry her eyes, think of something to say. "How long will she have to stay in the nursery?"

"If she lives and does very well, probably about three months. But she is not doing well now, she has not started to improve."

"I know. I know that she will die. Nature didn't want to have a child born that early live." Mrs. Martin was

preparing herself for her daughter's death in a way that I
had seen before and read about but could not really understand because I had never gone through it. There was
nothing to say or that needed to be said, and we sat in the
silent, dark room for a long time. While no words were
spoken, we shared uncounted indescribable feelings in our
own ways as our hands touched. When I left she said,
"Thank you, I mean really . . . thank you. I mean, even
if the baby dies, thank you."

Somewhere inside me I knew exactly what she was
saying, and I said, "You are welcome." I wanted to hug
her for the gift she had given me, but only the embarrassed
reply came out. I walked slowly back downstairs to the
nursery.

Alice was in a good mood, ignoring the almost certain
disaster that would soon come. She liked Pam and me, and
the three of us made a good team. As I walked in, she
handed me Baby Boy Brown, a healthy four-week-old
preemie who was doing well, just lying around the nursery,
gaining weight. He had been lucky to start out life weighing in at three and three-quarters pounds. "Feed Albie for
me, will you?" she said. Baby Boy Brown had been named
"Albie" by Alice for a reason that would be impossible for
me to explain, but made perfect sense at the time. Albie
was a beautiful baby.

Alice was mourning Phreddie in her own way. She
had worked here in the nursery, long before it became a
special care nursery. She had seen hundreds of children
die and had seen ten generations of interns and residents
learn to accept death as a reality of the job. Her way of
mourning Phreddie's death was to love even more those
babies who weren't going to die. And she wanted to teach
me to do the same. I should feed Albie and love Albie,
whom we had saved from death weeks ago; I should not
die with Phreddie Martin.

I fed Albie while Pam did some chores and Alice fed
another baby. We just sat there, watching the machine

breathe for Phreddie Martin. I would not be able to sleep, so Pam went into the call room, sleeping on the cot with her shoes on, stethoscope around her neck.

Every minute that the respirator was on at a pressure of thirteen was another minute passed. Time had run out on Phreddie; she would have to improve now or die. If her lung disease continued to worsen, she would die slowly; if she got a pneumothorax, she would die quickly.

As I fed the healthy child on my lap, I watched Phreddie's chest move in time with the sounds of the respirator. I began to mourn life not lived, the death of a friend I would watch while sitting in this chair.

(9)

One hour passed by without incident. Alice avoided Phreddie's table but sang to the other newborns. Carefully I drew out some blood, fearing Baby Martin as if she were nitroglycerin. Tillie's lights came alive—the blood oxygen had risen to ninety!

Without waiting for the other values, I ran back into the nursery, slowly approaching Phreddie's table and the deadly, life-giving machine beside it. I turned the pressure dial down to eleven and waited. Phreddie lay there unchanged, still keeping her pink, healthy color. She no longer needed the pressure of thirteen, the pressure that would rupture her lungs. But she had not had the pneumothorax, and now we were back down to eleven.

Fifteen minutes slowly passed and Alice came over as I repeated the blood gas. No words were spoken when I went in to Tillie and she told me the oxygen was forty-five, which was good. She had a good oxygen level at a pressure of eleven. She had begun to improve! She might live. . . . I kissed Tillie. Tillie the Terrific had given out good news for the first time in Phreddie's delicate life.

I returned, telling Alice the good news. She smiled and went back to her work. I stood by without getting my hopes up too high; it could change again. But the repeat oxygen had risen to fifty-eight, undeniable improvement. The pressure was no longer dangerous—Phreddie would live! As I walked in the nursery I wanted to jump for joy, and I realized that I could. I picked up Albie and began dancing around the nursery, singing "Home on the Range" as loud as I could. Albie looked up at me with a very dumb expression.

Pam ran in, confused, and I explained what had happened. Phreddie lay on the table, pink as ever, somehow looking much healthier to me. I began to relax, allowing all those feelings about Phreddie that I had secretly stored inside me to flow out. The hidden anguish turned to joy. Phreddie would live, I knew it now, Alice knew it. I never realized I could feel such joy in the nursery. Pam stole some coffee from the obstetrics floor, and making believe it was the finest French champagne, we toasted every baby in the nursery, waking each one and telling him or her the good news. Uniformly they responded with blank expressions, rolled over, and went back to sleep.

Two more hours passed and the oxygen had risen even further. We could lower the pressure to ten, well within the safe range. Phreddie lay still, the magic respirator keeping her alive as the hyaline membranes in her lungs began to disappear. I could now talk with Mrs. Martin.

Trying to control my enthusiasm and optimism, I told Mrs. Martin that her daughter was beginning to improve. She, of course, was not out of danger yet, but she had improved tremendously since the last time I had talked with her. She cried again, a different cry, and I cried too, hiding my tears, not understanding the overwhelming series of emotions that swept over me.

On the way back to the nursery I walked down the stairs whistling, probably the first time in history a pediatrician whistled with happiness at four in the morning.

When Emily and Steve came in three hours later, I casually told them that Phreddie Martin was better, the pressure down to ten. Although Phreddie was not ready to leave the hospital, we saw that the four of us, plus John, Dr. Williams, Alice and the other nurses, the lab and x-ray technicians, the secretaries, and everyone else had saved this baby's life. We had made it possible for Mr. and Mrs. Martin, after six years of trying to have children, to have a daughter.

(10)

Four days later we were able to disconnect the respirator and take out the endotracheal tube. We had stopped the morphine, and when the tube came out, Phreddie cried for the first time since the day she was born. She was a beautiful, small person, and although she still needed extra oxygen given through the hood, we took her off the danger list. She took her first bottle of formula, sucking it down like an experienced eight-month-old, using a preemie nipple. She had developed none of the other dangerous complications of prematurity.

She began to grow like a regular preemie who had not been sick. A month passed during which we all loved her, played with her, fed her. She was now Sarah Martin, her mother's chosen name replacing our affectionate "Phreddie." Sarah was a beautiful name for this child. We didn't think she looked much like Phreddie the fish anymore.

part iv
Stephen Benson

(1)

The nursery work always seemed endless and the repetition of daily minor tasks burdensome: doing blood tests for jaundice, looking at x-rays, doing physical exams, taking cultures for infection. But the routine was broken with new, unusual problems, things we had never seen before, never read about in textbooks. And the ever present tension of unexpected emergencies kept us alert. I was looking forward to the end of my rotation in the nursery, for it had been exhausting, and I needed the vacation of being on the emergency floor. There it was also busy, but seeing sixty children with colds and cuts seemed relaxing. Even the occasional true emergency was not as nerve-racking, for the children were older and stronger and they could tell us where it hurt.

It had been an ordinary day in the nursery, and that night both Pam and I got about four hours' sleep, for which we were very thankful. After a leisurely coffee-and-doughnut break, we went on our work rounds, carefully checking the progress of each child. The phone rang, and it was for me.

Gail was a close friend of mine, working as a surgical nurse in another hospital, and her call posed an unusual problem, one that I had never faced before. She had two friends who lived in a commune in the western part of the state, and they were planning to have their baby at home,

without medical supervision. Gail asked me if I would
go out to their house with her to talk with them and help
them prepare for the birth. I agreed, and we left early
Sunday morning.

We approached an old farm at the end of a dirt road.
The crops on the cleared land seemed to be flourishing.
Just over the door was a sign that read:

SAT NAM
Please Leave Shoes Outside

Underneath was a big pile of shoes to which we added
ours. Gail hugged her friends, Kristin and Peter, introduced me, and we went into the kitchen.

The farmhouse was neatly kept by the fifteen people
who were living there. Kristin brewed some red clover tea,
which she said would "purify my blood," and told me that
until recently she had been working in a nearby town,
teaching music. Peter spent most of his time on the farm,
feeding the animals and canning vegetables for the winter.
Kristin was about eight and one-half months pregnant,
and as I sat drinking tea, I thought the baby, or babies,
looked big. Kristin and Peter were kind, gentle people,
and I felt at ease with them immediately.

Peter asked me what Gail had told me.

"Not too much except that you are planning to have
your baby here," I answered, not exactly sure of what my
role was.

"We don't want to go into the hospital, and we feel
it would be perfectly safe here."

"Will an obstetrician be coming out?" I asked.

Kristin sipped her tea and paused. "I had prenatal
care with Dr. James in town, but neither he nor the other
doctors in town will make house deliveries. They say it is
not safe. Also, we had certain differences of opinion about
natural childbirth. We study and practice yoga here and
want natural childbirth. Dr. James doesn't understand
yoga and doesn't want to listen to us. He said we could
'try' natural childbirth, but only in the hospital. I don't
think he likes us very much."

"I'm sorry," I said.

"Also, we really can't afford it. It costs three hundred dollars for the obstetrician's fee and then the hospital costs. . . . We don't have much money. But money really isn't that important. What we want is to do what is best for our baby. He lives here, he should be born here with those who love him. Not in some cold, frightening hospital with medical students watching."

I saw that their decision to have the baby at home was firm. I really didn't want to talk them out of it, but I felt I should try. "Have you had a baby before?"

"No."

"Have you prepared for this?" I asked.

"As much as we could," Peter said. "We've read a couple of books and have scissors, clean sheets, and other things. The room upstairs is already prepared." The way Peter answered, I knew they had probably read every book they could find about childbirth. They weren't taking this whole baby thing lightly.

"No . . . I mean, have you prepared your minds for this?" The scissors and sheets were not at all important at this stage.

"What do you mean?" Kristin asked.

"Well, everybody in this country has her baby in the hospital. It's just the way it's done here. Whether you like it or not, you are alone in this decision, and what will happen to you if there are problems? If the baby were to die during delivery, would you spend the rest of your life in regret?"

"We have asked ourselves this question and believe that we have chosen the best way. Babies in other countries are born at home all the time."

"In other countries they are prepared for this, and usually a midwife or a doctor attends the birth. It can be pretty scary." I felt almost fatherly as I said this even though we were all the same age.

"Well," Peter began slowly, "babies have been born all the time, even before there were doctors. Nature provides for itself in this way. If the baby is sick, then this is nature's way of saying that the child should not live. I don't know how to explain this, but if the baby is born dead, we would not have murdered our baby just because he had not been born in the hospital."

"Do you love your baby?" I asked, not knowing if they would understand what I meant.

"Yes," Kristin answered immediately.

"I don't really know the baby yet," Peter answered, "and that's one of the reasons for having it at home. I mean, it's half my baby, and I want to be part of the birthing, to be with my child during its first moments of separate life."

"There's one thing I want you to understand," Kristin said. "We want to do everything possible for our baby. We don't want it to be unsafe, but we feel that it would be better for the child to be born at home."

We talked for a long time about many things, and I drank teas that would prevent headaches, relieve muscles, and do wonders for other parts of me. The people of the house talked a different medical language, one I had never heard. I wondered what could be in clover tea that purified blood—maybe penicillin. It did look sort of moldy. But they were not interested in chemicals; they had learned from their own experience and others' advice that herbal teas had certain effects. I saw a life-style around me that, although it was different from my own, was just as real. It was something that Kristin and Peter lived and believed in. I met the other people of the house, and it was clear that the whole house was involved in the coming birth: the Bensons weren't as isolated as I had thought. I liked all the people I met.

I had two alternatives. I could be like Dr. James and reject them for their difference, saying that what they were doing was dangerous and foolish, or I could try to adapt my knowledge of medicine to their way of life. I looked down at my bare feet and realized that I had already chosen. I would try to help them.

"My colleagues in medicine would say that what you are doing is dangerous and stupid," I said.

"What do you think?" Peter asked. I was afraid someone was going to ask that.

"I really don't know," I answered. "I have been taught, and know it to be true, that medical care has lowered both infant and maternal mortality. In other countries, where they are prepared to have home births, the mortality is lower than here, but that doesn't apply to this situation because you are in this country, not someplace else."

"What do you think?" Peter saw that I was leading up to something.

"Well, in all honesty, I think the chances of serious problems for either Kristin or the baby are much greater without medical care. But some place inside me I can understand what you are saying. Your interest is not in the mortality rates but in your baby, and you believe that the baby is best born here in a way in which you believe."

"We are not rejecting medical care entirely. It's just that we want advice, not orders, and we want to deliver the baby naturally." Kristin paused, then looked up. "Will you help us deliver the baby?"

I was stunned. "I am a pediatrician, not an obstetrician."

"You are a doctor," Kristin answered.

"But I have not delivered a baby since the third year of medical school," I protested, "and even then I did not know what I was doing. If any problems came up, I would not be able to handle them properly."

"But you could help us deliver the baby. You have seen deliveries before—we have not."

This was true. I had seen hundreds of babies born, but I just checked out the baby after it was delivered. I could help. My being there was obviously safer than my not being there, but if I agreed to help, was I encouraging something that I felt was unsafe?

"I could advise you," I said.

"That's all we could ask for. After all, Kristin is delivering the baby—no one can do that for her."

We all knew that a commitment had been made:

Gail and I would help them out with the delivery. All we had to do now was to come to certain understandings.

"O.K., I will help you in any way I can, but if I think you are doing something dangerous, I will not hesitate to tell you." I knew that honesty would not be a problem.

A lunch of brown rice and fresh vegetables was delicious, and the hours that passed were filled with talk about every aspect of childbirth. We agreed about certain things. For example, if the baby was having signs of fetal distress, or if the baby was having trouble being born, we would drive right away to the local hospital, which was fifteen minutes away. If the labor went past eighteen hours, we would go to the hospital; the eighteen hours was a compromise figure.

Kristin had always been in good health; her medical history was just about perfect except for a broken finger she had when she was ten. Her prenatal care was normal, no urine sugar or protein, normal blood pressure. Her blood type was O positive, and she had a negative syphilis test. She had never been pregnant before, and from the way she talked, she already loved this baby more than I could imagine. Dr. James had told her there were no twins and that everything appeared normal. I did not examine Kristin because I would have had no idea of what to look for. But her blood pressure was normal when I took it.

She would call both Gail and me at the first sign of labor or at the time her membranes ruptured, whichever should happen first. If her membranes ruptured before we arrived, she would save some of the fluid in a clean glass jar. If anything at all happened, she promised to call.

She asked me how much it would cost. The idea of charging money for something I had never done before, and had only shaky notions of, was absurd to me, so we agreed upon two free yoga lessons after the baby was born.

We were all happy—everyone in the house was happy. They had prepared themselves for a delivery without medical care present, but now they would have advice. I saw that my advice would be taken seriously, not because they were awed by it, but because they trusted me. By the time we had our final cup of tea, there were about twelve house members in the kitchen, and we felt like dancing. Gail and I sorted out our shoes from the pile and drove slowly home.

Gail and I felt good about helping the Bensons, but we were also frightened. Gail had seen only a couple of deliveries in nursing school, and I certainly didn't feel competent as an obstetrician. But we experienced a strange feeling of peace as we left the farm that Sunday. For a rare day off from the nursery, it had been well spent.

(2)

Steve and Emily were really quite excited, even though it was a Monday morning and they had been up all night. They were excited because I was going to do this and happy that they weren't. I was a little nervous, and I find it difficult to say why. I guess because, as a doctor, I should have demanded that which was safest. I think I had not done so because I agreed with them: babies, if all was well, and the appropriate arrangements were made, should be born at home as in other countries. I didn't realize this at first—I had never thought of it before.

It is a question of emphasis. The doctor's emphasis is on disease, because that is what his training and ability are oriented toward. There are hundreds of healthy babies born in our hospital and they go unnoticed by us. If they are healthy, they don't need us. We spend our time with the babies who are sick. Sick children are referred to us because of the special care nursery, but never healthy babies. We look at illness all the time; we think in terms of disease, not health. Of course, health is the goal, but it is considered only the absence of disease.

The Bensons have not had the same experiences I have had. They have never seen a sick infant, never seen a child die. They think in terms of health, recognizing illness as a real possibility, but having faith in what they call the "human organism" to be fundamentally healthy.

They were happy that Gail and I would be there because of the possibility of illness, but their desire to have the baby at home was due to health. If a normal baby were born, it would be healthier for him to be born without drugs, by natural childbirth, at home where he was loved. Who knows what the first moments of an infant mean? Perhaps the infant can somehow sense the atmosphere of pain and sorrow in the hospital in the same way that we know the fetus can be influenced while still inside the womb. Science does not consider these things. The Bensons believed strongly that the baby would be healthier if he were not born routinely in a hospital. It would be better for the child and the parents, for it would help establish a close love relationship right from the beginning. They believed this so strongly that they were willing to risk the possibility of complications. Kristin knew that she ran a greater risk of dying from hemorrhage, for she knew that I would be able to do little except rush her to a hospital, perhaps giving an injection that would help. But she recognized this risk and was willing to take it for her child. She felt it was the least she could do to make "everything right."

"But suppose everything isn't right?" I kept asking myself. I mean, that's my job, I'm supposed to think of these things. Of course, if there is no problem and it is a normal delivery, as happens 90 percent of the time, then everything will be fine. I will just stand around with little to do and give simple advice about the best way to cut the cord and keep the baby warm. But suppose there were problems? My mind couldn't handle that. Steve, Emily, and Pam would help me prepare.

I had made a commitment to the Bensons. I made it knowing what I was doing, and now I began working on that commitment. I had one or two weeks to prepare, if the baby came on the due date. I read about childbirth and its complications. I bought a book of obstetrics and, looking at the pictures, I was frightened even more, and you can't learn from pictures.

Emily got me a laryngoscope and an ambu bag on

loan. I gathered a handful of various-sized endotracheal tubes and put them carefully in the bag I was preparing. When Steve handed me the scope he mumbled something like "I hope you don't need this . . ." and his voice trailed away as he walked off. I hoped so too, but if, by any chance, the baby shouldn't breathe, with this equipment I would be able to keep him alive, hopefully, until we reached a hospital.

Monday morning was routine, yet busy enough so that we all were running around. Pam picked up some vitamin K and syringes when she was on the delivery floor and dropped them off in the bag. The growing bag became home plate for the day, and whenever we were not doing something else, we thought of the bag. Steve dropped in a few packages of sterile cord clamps and some ampoules of silver nitrate for the baby's eyes. Pam dropped in a couple of packages of suture material and some scalpel blades—I'm not sure why the latter, but I'd take them just in case. Lots of bandages and sterile towels, and the bag grew in size as everyone in the nursery concentrated on finding everything that could possibly be used. Baby Girl Carper, who was being discharged, donated her diaper pins, as her mother would use tape on diapers.

I hoped that Monday night would be quiet—maybe I could get some pointers from the obstetricians about doing a normal delivery, even learn a little about complications. It's hard to learn two years of obstetrics in one week, and eventually I decided that I could not become sophisticated in this; I wouldn't consider taking along forceps.

On visit rounds we talked about the situation. I explained the prospective birth to Dr. Williams in a way that showed I had no choice but to help these poor people in their time of need. He did not think home deliveries were a very good idea. I wanted to say that what they were doing was a great idea, but as I mentioned before, I am a coward, I have my future at stake. John and Dr. Williams gave me some pointers and we spent the hour talking about warning signs during labor. This time I listened very closely to what they had to say, resolving to do more reading about this.

At about four in the afternoon we got a call from the delivery room, asking us to come up and discuss a problem. To save our strength, Pam and I took the elevator.

(3)

Dr. Jane Pearson was the obstetrical resident on duty, and she told us that one of the women in the labor room had just ruptured her membranes and there was meconium in the amniotic fluid. She had been in labor for three hours and the baby was about thirty-eight weeks along, two weeks early.

I have always found the labor room very oppressive. There were about five women in various stages of labor at this time, ranging from the lady asleep in the end bed, moaning every few minutes, to the one in front of me, screaming with fear and pain. Pam and I looked at the name cards on the beds and found Mrs. Johnson. We introduced ourselves and explained our concern about the amniotic fluid.

I felt a little apprehensive because this is more unusual in a baby who is a bit early rather than late. The obstetrical nurse stated that the fetal heart rate was 120, but sometimes a little irregular. I explained to Mrs. Johnson that this was one of the signs the baby inside might be having some difficulty. Listening with the fetuscope over her stomach, I heard the irregularity: the beat would slow, then speed up. Over a minute's time the number of beats would be the normal 120, but the irregularity and the meconium staining was worrisome. Mrs. Johnson noticed my expression and asked, "Will the baby be all right?"

"I think so," I responded, "but these warning signs

indicate that there may be a problem. We would like to
monitor the baby's heartbeat during the contractions to
be sure it doesn't slow down. With the fetuscope, we cannot hear the fetal heart during a contraction, but with the
monitor we can. The machine is much like an EKG machine with one of the wires attached to the head of the
baby. This way, the machine will trace out the baby's
heartbeat at all times. If the heartbeat slows down during
the contractions, then this would show problems."

"What kind of problems?" Mrs. Johnson asked.

"Well, if there were a knot in the umbilical cord, for
example, and the blood was not reaching the baby properly, or if the umbilical cord were wrapped about the
baby's head." Pam and I explained as best we could, asking
her to trust us, to trust our beliefs as to what was best for
her baby. We went back to the office to talk with Jane
Pearson.

"I think she needs to be monitored," I said.

"Yes, the machine is on the way up." Jane would set
everything up, explaining it in detail to Mrs. Johnson.

Fifteen minutes later the machine was running at the
foot of the bed, one of the wires inserted in Mrs. Johnson's
vagina and attached to the top of the baby's head. As a
contraction began, the baby's heart rate remained steady,
and held at 130 per minute, but fell down to 80 moments
after the contraction ended. This probably meant that the
umbilical cord was being compressed by the bones of the
pelvis, slowing the blood supply to the baby. When an unborn infant is not getting an adequate supply of oxygen,
the heart rate drops. In this situation, to prevent possible
damage to the baby, a Caesarian section and immediate
delivery was, we felt, the safest alternative for the baby.

Pam and I went downstairs to prepare for a "bad
baby" while Jane explained the situation to Mr. and Mrs.
Johnson. They agreed to the Caesarian section, and minutes later Mrs. Johnson was wheeled into the operating
room of the delivery floor. She was soon under anesthesia
and the operation began.

Pam and I had changed into clean scrub suits, waiting

for the baby. While I waited, our equipment ready, my mind wandered over some vaguely remembered statistics. Without the operation there was a good chance that the baby would be all right, as there was no outward sign of damage, but there was also a chance the baby would be born dead. We were prepared for a "depressed baby," an infant who, because of oxygen deprivation while inside the womb, would not breathe on his entry into the new world that was awaiting him.

My thoughts lasted only a few moments, and as the infant girl was lifted from the opened abdomen of the mother, she began to cry. A few seconds later, the cord was cut and the baby was carefully handed to Pam. The baby was well; she would not need any of our specialized services. As we dried her off, we said hello, welcoming her to this new world, apologizing for the abruptness of the delivery, and thanking her for being so healthy. As she cried, the obstetricians went back to the surgical tasks before them, and Pam and I returned to the nursery.

From the first suspicion of a problem to its diagnosis and cure had taken about forty minutes. The umbilical cord had wrapped itself twice about the baby's neck, and as labor grew stronger, the pressure became greater. Perhaps, if labor had not been surgically interrupted, the baby would have died during the next six hours of labor. If there were complications of this kind with Kristin and Peter's baby, would we be able to get to the hospital in forty-five minutes? Then, of course, it would have taken another hour to get the operation under way because we would have to line up a surgeon, prepare the operating room, and so forth. If Kristin and Peter had been here today, would they still want to have their baby at home?

In other countries, where home deliveries are expected and planned for, there would have been little time lost in a situation such as this. An ambulance would have radioed ahead to begin preparations even before the patient arrived. But in this country, home deliveries are almost unheard of, especially in the cities, possibly because it is more profitable for the physicians to deliver babies in the hospital, takes less time for them there, or because the people here are afraid of what they would see at home. I think that home deliveries, if there is adequate protection, for those who want them, would be a big advance in American medicine. It works very well in other countries; perhaps we could start to catch up in the patient-care race.

I became nervous thinking about the Bensons' baby. If I saw these signs in Kristin, what would I do? Just the best I could, I guess. But Baby Johnson could have died without medical care. If this happened to Baby Benson because she was born at home, would I ever forgive myself for taking part and, to some limited extent, even supporting the venture? I could get her to a hospital, give her oxygen, try to get the obstetrician on call, and hope that they would get the personnel to do the C-section in time. But, as usual in situations like this, there is really no choice.

(4)

The week passed slowly as I waited for the call from Peter and Kristin. I had bought a small tank of oxygen from a local supply house, guaranteed for fifteen minutes of oxygen, which I hoped would forever remain in the tank. I had heard that cardboard boxes are good insulators, so I fashioned one into the shape of an incubator, softening it with towels. My little bag was overflowing with items I prayed I would not have to use.

I had arranged with a friend that if the call should come at a time when I was on duty he would cover for me, but this proved unnecessary. The call came at four in the afternoon, just before I was to leave for the night. I would be off until seven the next morning and hoped there would be time for a little sleep, maybe a short, three-hour labor. Peter was quite excited when he called: the contractions had started about an hour ago, and they were nice and steady now at about seven minutes apart. There had been no rupture of the membranes or leaking of blood or amniotic fluid, and it seemed that labor was off to a good start. I told him I would be out as soon as possible, and he said he had already talked with Gail and she would meet me there. As I hung up the phone, perspiration appeared on my hands. Pam smiled from across the room and said, "Good luck."

The drive out to the farm was uneventful, even with

rush-hour traffic. Not being too experienced in the length
of labors, I wondered if the baby would be born by the
time I got there. But "primips" (first pregnancies) had long
labors, so I drove slowly, hoping it would not be a long
night. I was thankful for the three hours of sleep I had
had the night before, even with my shoes on.

When I arrived, I noticed Gail's car and her shoes
in the pile by the door. After adding mine, I made my way
upstairs. There was no great bustle of activity in the room
as I entered, so I relaxed. Kristin looked comfortable, smiling, propped up by pillows that Peter was supporting.
They both said they were happy to see me, and I replied
that I was happy to have been invited. Indeed, it seemed
a different kind of labor than any I had ever seen: there
was an air of excitement, of happiness. I shared their feeling that an extraordinary event was about to take place.
It was being taken seriously and joyously by everyone in
the room. No one seemed to be nervous.

"Are you nervous?" I asked Kristin.

"Not really . . . well, maybe a little. I have never
done this before, you know." She was smiling and didn't
seem nervous to me.

"Are you nervous, Peter?" I asked.

"I guess I'm more nervous than Kristin is. I wish
there was more I could do. Are you nervous?" I was a little
surprised by his question.

"Maybe a little. I've never been invited to help a baby
get born at home before." But the tension had disappeared
from my face and voice, and I felt very much at ease in
the room. As they recognized my ease, their confidence
rose. There was a doctor here now, it's all right. But I
wanted to be certain they were set on their actions, and in
addition to repeating my own inexperience again, I asked,
"Are you sure you want to have the baby here instead of
the hospital?"

"We are sure." There was no pause of doubt, no trace
of insecurity in their voices. They both smiled, and I
smiled.

"O.K.," I said, "that's that. Now, how is your labor coming?"

Peter answered after picking up a little notebook that was on the table beside the bed. He had timed the contractions, writing accurately the intervals between each. The last one was about five minutes ago and had lasted twenty seconds. "They have been coming every seven or eight minutes apart, and pretty strong."

Besides Gail, there were three other people in the room: Martha, Adrian, and Julia. It seems that the household members had discussed who would be in the room at the time of the delivery and who would wait outside. It wasn't that they weren't welcome, but twenty people in the room would have been too much of a crowd. Everything had been thought of and the room was very neat, with tables holding neatly arranged supplies. I picked a corner of the room for my equipment.

Kristin was beginning to have a contraction. She set her teeth and closed her eyes, but still kept the faint smile on her lips. She was breathing slowly and evenly, and the contraction was strong, lasting thirty-five seconds. She relaxed when it ended and looked as fresh as ever. Labor was indeed under way.

Kristin's blood pressure and pulse were normal, and the fetal heart rate through the fetuscope was normal at about 140 and regular. The membranes had not ruptured and everything seemed to be going smoothly.

Downstairs in the kitchen there was a lot of activity. Tea, which was said to be good for labor, was being prepared, but I asked for some regular old instant coffee, hoping they had some and that I would not be insulting them. They kept some for guests and after a five-minute search found the jar. I was not going to have the baby—I didn't see why I needed the tea. But I did want to stay awake, and coffee is a well-known friend to me for that.

I found Harry, who had been designated "ambulance driver," and introduced myself. He had the van filled with gas and had arranged a stretcher to make it more comfortable for Kristin, should she need it. He had learned the route to the hospital by heart. I was glad Harry was taking his job as seriously as everyone else, for in a pinch, he would be more important than I.

I called the local hospital and asked to speak to the physician in charge of the accident floor for the day. I introduced myself to Dr. Cohen, explaining that we were having a home birth and that if there were any problems we would be coming into the hospital. He was a little confused at first. I explained again that there was going to be a baby born at home, not in the hospital. I put it in such a matter-of-fact way he did not bother to question it. "Oh, I see . . . a home delivery, yes . . ." I said that if there were any problems with the labor or delivery I would be giving him a call or would come in if there were lacerations that needed suturing. He was still a little confused when we said good-by, but he would put it together. At the very least he would have a warm incubator ready. I did not explain to him that I was not an obstetrician; fortunately he did not ask. I wasn't a general practitioner, either, but a specialist in another field altogether. But I had succeeded in one thing: if there were problems that necessitated our going to the hospital, Dr. Cohen would not be taken completely by surprise.

I talked with some of the people in the house while I was drinking my coffee. Everyone was excited about the birth and taking on responsibilities that friends and families do not ordinarily take. Usually Mother goes away and comes back home with a neatly groomed baby. But here everyone had a role, a responsibility. Harry's was easy; he had a concrete job that he could prepare for and carry out. Others had less easily defined roles but were united in their love and support of Kristin and Peter.

One boy, Tom, had nothing to do but be there. His presence was the only thing he could offer. But he had to examine even this role carefully. If, for example, both Kristin and the baby died during the delivery, in such a way as could have been prevented in a hospital, would he feel guilty about not having expressed his doubts strongly enough beforehand? That was a difficult question, one which everyone in the household, including me, had to come to terms with in his own personal way.

The coffee was wonderful, and in my mind I decided I was an obstetrician. But I did not tell anyone.

(5)

Over the next hour, the contractions became stronger, lasting thirty seconds and coming about five minutes apart. Labor was picking up. Kristin was looking well and strong, talking in between the contractions to those in the room, not denying that she was in pain, but accepting it and concentrating on the beauty of the natural process. She was saving her strength for what she knew would come. Peter was kneeling at the top of the bed, supporting the pillows that Kristin leaned against. She was in a half-sitting position that she found comfortable, and Peter was wiping her brow with a damp facecloth, giving his wife some ice chips to chew between contractions. She had a little tea, and everyone was relaxed, waiting for the completely predictable miracle that nature had planned.

There was not too much talking. Occasionally Julia would go outside to get a fresh washcloth and Adrian would play the guitar and sing slow, quiet songs. The time passed slowly, but there was no hurry. Gail and I took turns watching Kristin's blood pressure and taking the fetal heart rate every fifteen minutes or so.

I explained to Kristin that it would be important to examine her vaginally during the labor to see how the baby was descending through the birth canal. She agreed and so, using sterile gloves and an antiseptic solution, I felt for the bones of her pelvis and the baby's unborn head.

I tried to remember from medical school all the important things to look for. The baby's head was "engaged," which meant it was no longer floating free within the uterus but was descending into the pelvis. This was important for several reasons. First, it told us that the baby would be coming out headfirst and wouldn't be a breech delivery, or in some other position, for which I breathed a sigh of relief. Also, when the head is engaged it is almost impossible for the umbilical cord to slip down and get wedged between the bones of the pelvis and the baby's skull, thus cutting off the baby's blood supply, something that is called a "prolapsed cord."

I could feel the cervix of the uterus, a thick muscular outlet of the womb. Usually this opening is only tiny, but with the pressure of the baby bearing down, the cervix had begun to stretch open, now being about two or three centimeters wide. As labor continued, the cervix would stretch so the baby's head would fit through. I recognized, probably for the first time, what a beautiful, simple process childbirth is, the mechanism evolving through thousands of generations, effective enough to ensure the continuation of this beautiful, but sometimes dangerous, species called man.

Kristin and Peter had recognized this long before I had, even though medicine was my profession. This knowledge was the reason they wanted their child born at home, using medical science where it could be helpful, but not substituting it for a completely natural process. Kristin recognized also that pain was a part of labor, and with this recognition and her own courage she overcame her fear. Without the fear, she was easily able to stand the pain, to accept it as an uncomfortable sensation and as a message telling her that her child would soon be born. She had no need for narcotic drugs, as these drugs do not lessen the pain but only the fear associated with it. With narcotics, the sensations of pain are still recognized, but because anxiety and fear are reduced, the pain seems different and not as acute. Kristin had no need for scopolamine or other drugs that make one forget about the experience, for she wanted to live the childbirth, become part of it, not forget it as an unwanted, unpleasant experience. This was the birth of her first child, perhaps the most important event in her child's life, and she wanted to share it and do whatever she could for her child; she did not want to forget.

The process of childbirth is not foolproof, but it works pretty well. If it didn't, mankind, as we know it, would not exist. It is amazingly simple, yet science knows little about it. After nine months of pregnancy, there is some signal for labor to begin. Then, gently at first, the body rhythmically begins to push the baby out from the uterus. As labor progresses the contractions get stronger and more frequent, and the baby is born. It is not known if there are any changes in an infant who does not go through a complete labor. For example, Baby Johnson was born by a Caesarian section: does this have an effect upon what kind of a person she will be when she grows up? But this, of course, is an academic question, for without the C-section she might not have had the opportunity to grow up. But medical science does not have the answers to questions raised by some of its actions. Maybe some day all deliveries will be done by C-section; they are much faster that way.

When I finished the vaginal exam, I explained to Kristin what I had felt. But she needed no further proof that the baby was being born, for she had another contraction, this one lasting forty seconds. She began to breathe hard, maintaining control of her body and the pain. She was not frightened.

Gail and I went downstairs to an empty room and discussed what we would do at the time of the delivery. We opened up the tank of oxygen and found out how to work it. I explained in detail the procedure to follow in the event the baby did not breathe after being born. During the previous hour, while we were talking with Kristin and Peter, we had not talked about such things, but it was our job and training to be ready for such things, and now we discussed in detail our actions in the event of an emergency—the dosages of drugs, how to try to stop a hemorrhage.

While we talked, I became aware that Gail was thinking some of the same things I was: that we were witnessing something we had never seen in a hospital, a child being born in an atmosphere of love and caring. I wondered if the baby would somehow recognize this and, as Kristin and Peter believed, be a better, happier person because of it. I hoped so, for if all went well, this child would have a beautiful, excellent start to life. Our talk was professional, but our minds wandered off to thoughts about the beauty of nature following its course. We went upstairs, prepared for the worst possible events, but expecting and ready to share the experience that we were to witness.

The hours passed and labor became intense. About midnight, Kristin's membranes broke, and a gush of clear, straw-colored fluid came from her vagina. The amniotic fluid, which had surrounded the infant for nine months, had no meconium in it and smelled clean, with no signs of infection. I repeated the vaginal exam, and her cervix had dilated further. I could feel the soft spots on the baby's head, determining from these spots that the baby would be coming out face down, the normal presentation. Again, everything was progressing normally, nature working steadily, efficiently. We would only observe, for when nature is working well, you don't interfere.

The hours of labor began to show on Kristin's face. She was tired; she no longer talked between contractions but rested, trying to sleep. Julia, kneeling on the bed, sang to her in a quiet voice as the hours passed, songs that spoke of joy and love. Kristin was very strong, perhaps from years of practicing yoga, and although she was tired, her body held the strength of many more hours of labor, should that be needed. Kristin began to realize one of the fundamental laws of childbirth: once it has started it will not stop until the function is completed. You cannot turn off labor just because you are tired. The contractions continued to gain in strength, but her smile told me she was accepting the exhaustion in the same way she accepted the pain. She was not frightened by her exhaustion; she even seemed to welcome it, for it was another sign that the child was being born.

The contractions were coming frequently, about every three minutes, and were lasting forty-five seconds. They were so much stronger than four hours earlier that they seemed entirely different. During them Kristin would pant hard, not pushing down, but breathing very hard while trying to relax the rest of her. Her cervix was almost completely dilated and opened now, and the head would be descending soon. The baby's heartbeat was strong and regular, and Kristin's blood pressure remained normal.

We began to make ready for the baby. I put a hot-water bottle in the cardboard box incubator to warm up the towels that were inside. My equipment was ready on the table in the corner. The scissors, clamps, and other instruments had been boiled for sterilization. We placed a clean, dry pad under Kristin's naked body to absorb the amniotic fluid that was still leaking out, and brought out the other clean sheets that would be needed. Using sterile gloves and an antiseptic cleaning fluid, Gail carefully washed off Kristin's bottom while I showered and washed up. Peter and Gail also showered, and we put on some clean "delivery room" clothes that I had borrowed from the hospital. Kristin recognized that the time was soon coming and began to recover her strength.

After a particularly strong contraction, Kristin said, "I feel like pushing now." She smiled through the perspiration on her exhausted face.

"I guess the baby is ready to come out," I said, returning her smile.

(6)

I explained to Kristin that she could push a little bit, but she should not try to push the baby out too rapidly. Her vagina was small, and it would take a little time and patience to stretch it so it would not rip as the baby passed through. I would tell her when to push and when not to, but it would be difficult for her to resist the urge to push. To avoid this urge, she would concentrate even harder on panting during the contractions. Again, she would rest between the contractions.

During the next few contractions she was pushing down hard, holding her breath, and forcing the baby through the cervix of her uterus. Soon the wet, black hair of the baby's head showed to the outside from the ring her vagina made. At this time she would try not to push at all for the next couple of contractions, for her vagina had to stretch. We placed a sterile towel under her bottom and one towel to cover each leg. Another towel would be used to receive the baby. Adrian supported Kristin's back and Julia held a mirror so the mother could see the hair of her about-to-be-born infant. Peter and I put on sterile gloves. During the next contraction Kristin panted hard, wanting to cry out from the pain, but instead concentrated on not pushing down. The pressure of the contraction itself pushed the baby forward slightly, stretching open the small vagina. One minute later, and again the stretching.

The beads of perspiration gathered on Peter's forehead as he waited for his child, carefully not touching anything with his sterile gloves.

Finally, the vagina had stretched enough, and with a push the infant's head came out. Peter held the head and slowly guided out the shoulders and body of his son. The wet, warm slippery body began to move, and after a cough, he began to cry. Kristin sat up, looking down between her legs with amazement at the new life that had come forth. Peter and Kristin began crying, sobbing with joy as their son moved about, flexing his arms, opening his eyes, looking around for the first time.

The child had been born and was well. The door opened and the other house members came in, everyone laughing, crying, hugging each other, rejoicing, and welcoming the new child. The room was full as Peter, tears in his eyes, began to tie off the umbilical cord with the sterile twine we had brought. Carefully placing two ties together about one inch from the baby and another four inches away, he picked up the scissors and cut between the ties, and the child was separated from his mother. Still overcome with joy, he dried the baby, handing him carefully to Kristin, and they cried together for the joy of the new life they had produced. Their son was not crying but moving about, carefully studying this strange new world in the arms of his loving parents.

The baby was pink and vigorous; there would be no problems. Gail and I stood back as the house members gathered around the new parents showing their love. I had never seen life this beautiful: I had never seen the joy of two new parents as a part of them became independent life. Everyone in the house was sharing this joy. I continued to watch the infant from across the room, knowing I would not need all the equipment I had brought. He was born at 1:55 in the morning, and someone left the room to figure out the new child's astrological chart.

I had been watching Kristin also. There did not seem to be much bleeding, and after a few minutes I examined her vagina carefully, looking for lacerations and tears. There were a few tiny cuts, but nothing large enough to cause any problems, none large enough to require sutures. The stretching had worked well. After another fifteen minutes the placenta delivered intact, after Peter and I put very gentle pressure on the cord to pull it out during a contraction. There were no torn pieces left inside that could cause problems later. There was no bleeding of consequence, and Kristin's uterus became hard and started to shrink in size.

I asked Peter, "How is your son?"

"Stephen. That's his name . . . Stephen. He's beautiful," Peter said through his tears. He handed Stephen to me.

As I held the child, I noticed that in one sense he looked like the thousands of other healthy babies I had seen, but in another sense he looked quite different. He sort of looked happy as he moved slowly, exploring his new world. He looked like his parents and seemed to share their sense of peace. I listened to his heart, and the beat was strong and regular. I handed Stephen back to his parents, saying, "He's beautiful."

Gail stayed in the room, and I took a walk around the farm, always staying within earshot. This is where Stephen would spend his early years, learning to walk and talk, coming to know and love his parents as they would come to know and love him. I spent half an hour in the silence of the night, trying to understand just what it was that I had seen. I was never able to put it into words, but I recognized it as one of the most beautiful experiences of my professional life. I did not need to conquer some devastating illness to feel a strong bond with my patient. This was a regular healthy child, like thousands of others, part of the beautiful mystery of life.

By three in the morning, life began returning to normal. Some of the house members went off to sleep, preparing to go to work the next day. Kristin was breast-feeding the child, and the room was cleaned up. Peter, Kristin, and I talked for a long time about children, what sort of experiences they would have as parents, how they would have to share their joys and frustrations. Kristin was no longer tired, her energy returned, and the joy showed as she handled and fed her son. I made a complete physical examination of Stephen, explaining everything in detail to the new parents. I wanted them to understand about their child, how to take care of the cord until it fell off, and so on. After a long discussion, we placed some antibiotic drops in Stephen's eyes to prevent a gonorrhea eye infection, should the parents happen to have gonorrhea. They objected at first, saying they did not have the infection, but because the risk of blindness was present, and because I felt strongly that it should be done, they agreed. We decided against giving Stephen a shot of vitamin K.

Stephen was dropping off to sleep when we had our toast with a special-occasion wine. When Gail and I collected our shoes at the front door, I again saw the sign that said "Sat Nam." This was a term that meant "Go in peace" or "Come in peace." I was happy for the love that Stephen would experience during his first few years here—a love that began here and could never have been replaced by all the fancy modern machines of our nursery. But I was also pleased that, if Stephen Benson had needed Tillie's specialized services, the love the parents felt would still have been there.

A child has been born: a child not unlike any of the hundreds of other children born that day throughout the world. And like other children, Stephen had been loved intensely ever since the first time he moved inside Kristin's abdomen, a love that grew along with the child. Their decision to deliver the baby at home was at first very foreign to me, but I began to discover what they were saying. Peter and Kristin live and believe in a philosophy which I do not understand but now respect. They wanted to live their life in love and wanted their child to become part of, and share in, that love right from the very first moments of life. They saw this as impossible in a hospital, where Baby Boy Benson would have been labeled and tucked neatly in a corner crib of a well-ordered nursery and transient nurses would prop a bottle in his mouth every four hours and change his diapers every two hours.

The experience of a child probably begins long before the child can think in a human way. It begins with conception and continues uninterrupted throughout pregnancy and childhood into adult life. At some level of unconscious life, birth may be an individual's most important experience, to which all other experiences are added. Who is to say?

But if what Peter and Kristin believe is true, then Stephen had the best possible start in life. Although I know as a pediatrician that it is physiologically impossible, I thought I saw Stephen smile with thanks when he was born.

I would return in two weeks to the farm for my first free yoga lesson.

(7)

In the nursery at seven o'clock that morning, Pam and Steve asked me how it went.

"It was nice. The baby was fine." I was once again in the other world where my feelings would diffuse out to the thirty patients in the nursery. There was no way to communicate what had happened. There is no way to measure feelings and love. In the nursery we talked the language of numbers, values, diagnoses. Information relates to the concrete, that which can be statistically interpreted and analyzed. How could I tell Steve how beautiful the experience had been? I would have to describe it as an APGAR of 10. (APGAR is a scoring system for newborns, the value 10 being perfect health.)

What I had seen had no place in our nursery; it was anti-nursery. It was almost anti-medicine, for there was no prestige involved in a completely normal, uncomplicated childbirth. It wouldn't be worth mentioning to John.

But to Kristin and Peter, I was a physician who helped them with the birth of their son. The presence of Tillie the Terrible, with all her accurate numbers, would not have made the Bensons feel at all comfortable.

Stephen Benson and all the babies I saw in the nursery shared a common bond: they were newborns. But they were different in so many inexplicable ways.

Glossary of Medical Terms

Alveoli: microscopic air sacs in the lungs through which oxygen is exchanged for carbon dioxide.

Ambu bag: a softball-sized plastic bag which is used to push air. One end connects to an oxygen tank, the other to either a face mask or an endotracheal tube.

Amniotic fluid: clear, straw-colored fluid within the amniotic membranes which surrounds the fetus during intrauterine life.

Amniotic membranes: strong, thin, transparent membranes which surround the fetus while in the womb.

Anemia: low concentration of red blood cells within the blood.

Anoxia: oxygen deprivation.

Apnea: the absence of breathing.

Apnea monitor: a machine which sets off an alarm if the patient stops breathing.

Bicarbonate: a drug often used to counteract the accumulation of acid in the blood.

Bilirubin: a breakdown product of blood cells which is usually cleared from the blood by the liver.

"Bili lights": fluorescent lights which reduce the concentration of bilirubin.

Caesarian section: surgical delivery of an infant through the abdomen of the mother.

Cardiac massage: the pressing over the heart in order to

create a heartbeat in the absence of a normal heartbeat.

Cardiac output: the amount of blood pumped by the
heart in one minute.

Cerebral palsy: the aftereffects of birth damage to the
brain.

Cervix: the lowermost part of the uterus.

Chest tubes: large tubes which, in case of a pneumothorax,
will attempt to re-expand the lungs.

EKG: a machine that monitors the heartbeat visually on
an oscilloscope.

Electroencephalogram: a machine that records the electrical potentials of the brain. Commonly known as
the "brain wave" test, or EEG.

Endotracheal tube: a small tube which, when placed in
the trachea, delivers air directly to the lungs.

Epinephrine: A drug used as an asthma medication and
as a heart stimulant. Adrenaline.

Fellow: a doctor who, having completed internship and
residency, continues in hospital study in one of the
subspecialties.

Fetal distress: various signs which indicate that labor and
delivery are not going normally.

Fetuscope: a special stethoscope designed to convey the
fetal heartbeat through the mother's abdomen.

Hematocrit: a blood test comparing the volume of packed
red blood cells to the volume of plasma which is cell-
free. A normal hematocrit is from 35 to 45. Hemato-
crits below 30 indicate an anemia.

Hyaline membrane disease: a disease of premature babies
due to the immaturity of lung tissue.

Intracranial hemorrhage: bleeding within the skull or
cranium.

Jaundice: a yellow color of the skin and eyes caused by
the chemical bilirubin.

Kernicterus: a disease of the brain caused by the toxic
action of too high a concentration of bilirubin (jaundice). More likely to appear in premature babies.

Laryngoscope: a special flashlight that holds the mouth open and allows visualization of the vocal cords. Often used while passing an endotracheal tube between the vocal cords.

Meconium: the thick, black-green substance which fills the alimentary tract of the fetus. Usually eliminated in first few days after birth.

Neonatology: a subspecialty within pediatrics which deals exclusively with the care of newborns.

Placenta: a fetal organ which delivers oxygen into the baby's blood and releases waste products.

Pneumothorax: the collapse of a lung.

Respirator: a machine that assumes control of the patient's breathing, delivering air or oxygen to the lungs via an endotracheal tube at appropriate intervals.

Resuscitation: the attempt to bring a patient back to life after a major bodily injury or other emergency.

Scrub suits: clean white linen suits worn in the nursery in an attempt to prevent outside infections from entering the nursery.

"Scut work": routine chores.

Silver nitrate: antibiotic drops placed routinely in babies' eyes to prevent gonorrhea eye infections in the newborn.

Spinal fluid: fluid which normally surrounds the brain and the spinal cord.

Spinal tap: inserting a needle into the spine to collect some of the spinal fluid.

"Stat": emergency.

Surfactant: a chemical necessary to maintain patency of the alveoli.

Term baby: an infant born after a full forty-week gestation, a nine-month pregnancy.

Trachea: the "windpipe," connects directly with the lungs.

Umbilical cord: the jelly-like connection between the fetus and the placenta, containing two arteries and one vein.

Visit rounds: a one-hour daily discussion with the visiting professor about patient problems.

Vitamin K: a vitamin often given as an injection soon after a baby is born to prevent a bleeding disorder which sometimes occurs without the vitamin.

Work rounds: interns and residents examining each baby to check for progress or signs of illness.